IN COLD BLOOD

ADAM CROFT

BLACK CANNON
PUBLISHING

First published in Great Britain in 2021.

This edition published in 2022 by Black Cannon Publishing.

ISBN: 978-1-912599-77-6

Copyright © Adam Croft 2021

The right of Adam Croft to be identified as the author of this work has been asserted by him in accordance with the Copyright, Designs and Patents Act 1988.

All rights reserved. No part of this book may be reproduced in any form or by any electronic or mechanical means, including information storage and retrieval systems, without written permission from the author, except for the use of brief quotations in a book review.

This is a work of fiction. Names, characters, businesses, places, events, locales, and incidents are either the products of the author's imagination or used in a fictitious manner. Any resemblance to actual persons, living or dead, or actual events is purely coincidental.

A CIP catalogue record for this book is available from the British Library.

Printed and bound in Great Britain by Clays Ltd, Elcograf S.p.A.

MORE BOOKS BY ADAM CROFT

RUTLAND CRIME SERIES

1. What Lies Beneath
2. On Borrowed Time
3. In Cold Blood
4. Kiss of Death

KNIGHT & CULVERHOUSE CRIME THRILLERS

1. Too Close for Comfort
2. Guilty as Sin
3. Jack Be Nimble
4. Rough Justice
5. In Too Deep
6. In The Name of the Father
7. With A Vengeance
8. Dead & Buried
9. In Too Deep
10. Snakes & Ladders

PSYCHOLOGICAL THRILLERS

- Her Last Tomorrow
- Only The Truth
- In Her Image
- Tell Me I'm Wrong
- The Perfect Lie
- Closer To You

KEMPSTON HARDWICK MYSTERIES

1. Exit Stage Left
2. The Westerlea House Mystery
3. Death Under the Sun
4. The Thirteenth Room
5. The Wrong Man

All titles are available to order from all good book shops.

Signed and personalised editions available at adamcroft.net/shop.

Foreign language editions of some titles are available in French, German, Italian, Portuguese, Dutch and Korean. These are available online and in book shops in their native countries.

EBOOK-ONLY SHORT STORIES

- Gone
- The Harder They Fall
- Love You To Death
- The Defender

To find out more, visit adamcroft.net

HAVE YOU LISTENED TO THE RUTLAND AUDIOBOOKS?

The Rutland crime series is now available in audiobook format, narrated by Leicester-born **Andy Nyman** (Peaky Blinders, Unforgotten, Star Wars).

The series is available from all good audiobook retailers and libraries now, published by W.F. Howes on their QUEST and Clipper imprints.

W.F. Howes are one of the world's largest audiobook publishers and have been based in Leicestershire since their inception.

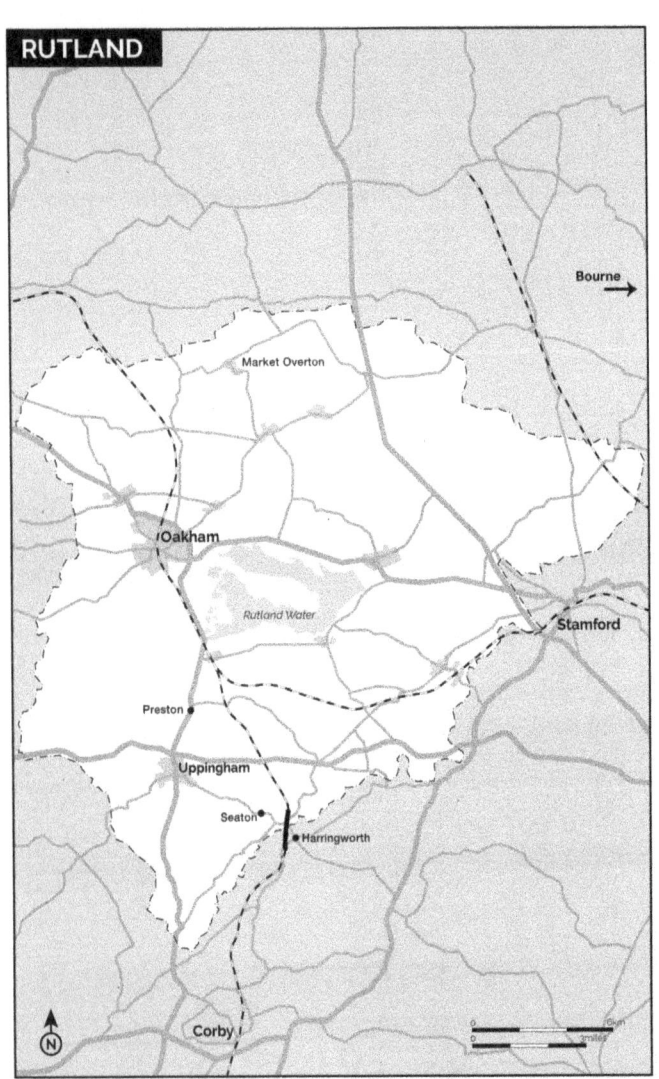

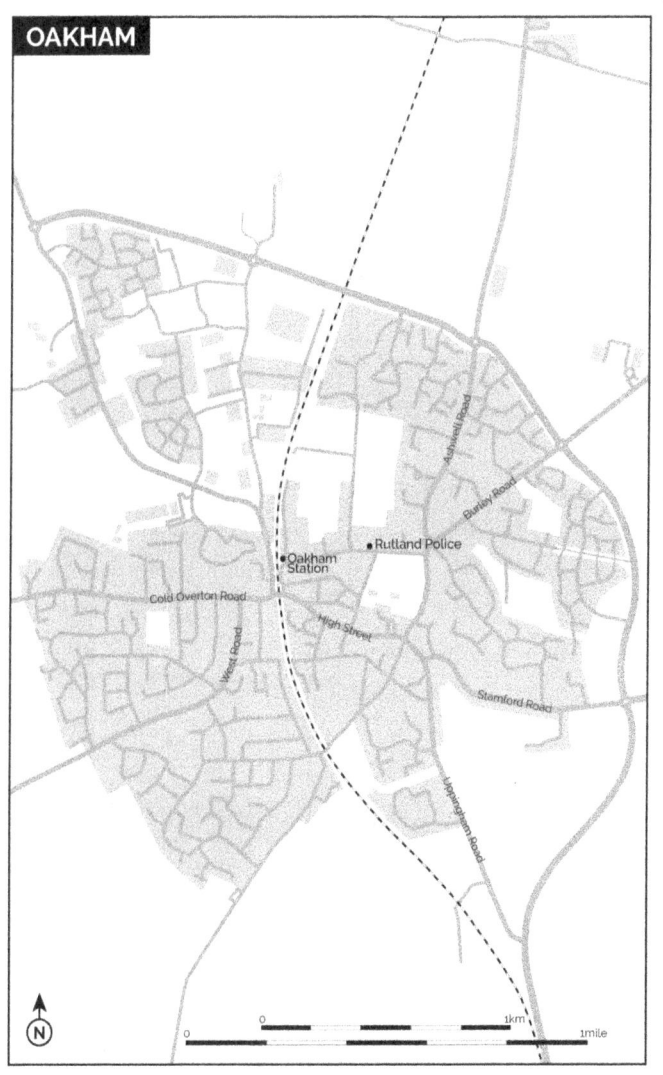

1

Sean Taylor thrust his hands into his coat pockets, willing them to warm up again. He'd only taken them out for a matter of seconds to help Millie put her scarf back on, but it was baltic. The fields and meadows, usually green, were a whiteish-grey, the morning frost still heavy, crunching underfoot.

He pulled his own scarf back over his chin and mouth, feeling his beard slowly defrosting as he did so. Still, he'd promised Ciara and the girls an early morning walk, and that's exactly what they were getting.

He didn't mind too much, but he doubted he'd have suggested it without Ciara's nudging. She tried a different health kick every new year, and 2021 wasn't going to be any different. He was just astounded she'd made it to February this time, and had to admit that frosty walks were preferable to the cabbage soup diet she'd inflicted on them last year.

She was convinced the cold weather meant her body had to work harder to keep her warm, and that more blood would be drawn to the muscles, making her heart pump harder and faster, thus helping her lose more weight. Sean wasn't entirely convinced as to the scientific basis behind that, but it was easier to smile and nod. After all, at least it wasn't cabbage soup.

He watched as Millie and Mia sprinted across the cold, hard ground of Seaton Meadow, wondering where they got their energy from. It took him at least three hours and twice as many cups of coffee to feel even vaguely alert. Still, he and Ciara had both been able to get the half-term week off work, so he supposed he should be thankful for small mercies.

'I don't know where they get their energy from,' Ciara said, as if reading his mind.

'I know. Certainly isn't from me.'

The girls looked up at the sound of a train soaring across the enormous Harringworth Viaduct, which intersected the meadow. It was a relatively rare sight, with only three trains passing over the viaduct on a busy day — and sometimes none at all. But it was always worth dragging the family out of bed to catch the sight of the 9.26 from Corby to Oakham soaring over Britain's longest masonry viaduct, splitting the meadow in half in glorious style.

Officially, the area was called Seaton Meadows — two s's — because of it. Sean had always considered it to be one field, especially as the train line was twenty-odd metres above them and there was absolutely nothing stopping people walking easily between the two meadows through any of the dozen arches. And what was the difference between a field and a meadow, anyway? Still, he was sure there were locals that would argue until they were blue in the face that it was, in fact, two meadows and not one field.

He'd even heard some people calling the northern section the Seaton Viaduct, arguing that they couldn't call that bit the Harringworth Viaduct like everyone called the rest of it, seeing as Harringworth was over the border in Northants and this bit was in Rutland. He could see their point, but took great pleasure in annoying both camps by only ever referring to it under its official, neutral name: the Welland Viaduct. With the River Welland forming the border between the two counties, it seemed to Sean to be the only logical moniker.

'They'll be knackered by the time we get home,' Ciara said. 'Should make for a quieter day than the last couple.'

'Fingers crossed. I was half thinking about washing the car, but I think I might give that a miss if it's going to stay like this. I might just sit with my hands and feet in the warm water instead. Girls, not too far please!'

Millie and Mia slowed down and waited for their parents to catch up, the morning mist thick, making it difficult to see more than a hundred yards at best. The last thing they needed was for one of them to disappear out of sight or, worse, tread in dog shit. It would be just their luck to find the one fresh steaming turd that hadn't yet frozen solid.

Sean glanced at his watch. They'd been walking around for almost half an hour. 'Shall we get back?' he asked, fully expecting Ciara to give him a look and tell him something about her VO2 max or heart rate variability.

'Good idea,' she replied, her lips almost the colour of a Smurf.

'Girls, come on. We're going to head back to the car. Your mum's about to turn into a block of ice.'

'How? I'm boiling!' Mia, the eldest, called.

'Yeah, well, you're practically mummified and you haven't stopped running about all morning. Spare a thought for us crusty old dudes over here.'

'Ugh, Dad. Don't use words like that, *pur-lease*.'

'Don't tell me "dude" has gone out of fashion now.'

'Only in, like, nineteen forty-six. No, I mean "crusty". It's revolting.'

Sean looked at Ciara as they shared a sympathetic look. 'She's nine, right? I mean, I didn't just blink and lose ten years?'

'Nope. She's nine. Scariest thing is, Millie'll be next. And sooner, probably, as she'll copy her sister.'

Sean sighed. 'Great. Can't wait.'

To their credit, the girls both waited by the gate at the edge of the meadow, leading onto the B672. They'd parked just on the other side of the road, in a makeshift parking area under the arches of the viaduct. There were usually a few dog walkers or families parked up, but the weather and ridiculously early hour meant the Taylors had been, and still were, the first car there. Sean felt pretty sure it'd be a good hour or two before anyone else bothered, either.

The four of them crossed the road — the girls choosing to run — and made their way onto the parking area. The girls carried on running, weaving in and out of the arches, chasing each other like a pair of wailing banshees.

'Come on, girls. In the car,' Sean called, unlocking the family's Vauxhall Meriva. 'Whack the heater on, love. Bloody windscreen's started to freeze again already.'

Before he could call over to Millie and Mia again, he was stopped dead in his tracks by an ear-piercing, blood-curdling scream. Without hesitation, he sprinted towards it. A few seconds later, he saw both his daughters and realised they were safe. They hadn't screamed because they were hurt. They'd screamed because of what they'd seen.

Both girls were rooted to the spot, staring with horror at the wall of one of the arches. As Sean followed their eyes, his own blood turned cold. Propped against the wall, as blue-grey as the paintwork on their car, eyes cloudy and frozen with a layer of frost, was the dead body of a man.

2

Caroline Hills sat down at her desk and opened her email inbox. She was glad she'd just had a few days off, because she was feeling tired enough as it was.

If she'd thought the exhaustion from chemotherapy had been bad, nothing could have prepared her for how absolutely bloody knackered she was following the hysterectomy. The six weeks off work had been hellish from a psychological point of view, but physically she knew they'd been necessary. The doctors had told her how much energy the recovery would take, but she'd presumed they were just being overly cautious. That was until she'd realised that even making a cup of tea had felt like running five circuits of Rutland Water.

If she was honest with herself, she struggled to remember the last time she'd had any real energy. The family's move to Rutland had been intended to re-energise and invigorate them all, but the timing couldn't have been worse. She just hoped they were now through the worst of it and that things would start to look up for them all.

Her recovery from the operation meant Christmas at home was a given, and it had the added benefit that Mark'd had to do all of the cooking and preparations. Still, Christmas seemed a long time ago now, and it wouldn't be long before they were looking forward to their summer holiday. Based on the arctic conditions she'd experienced that morning, though, summer seemed a whole lot further away than it really was.

Everything looked so bleak in the winter, and she found it hard to even visualise what things looked like in July. Just walking through her frozen back garden to the compost heap earlier that morning, it seemed impossible to even imagine she'd be sitting out in the sun just a matter of weeks later. Not that she'd ever get the time or five minutes' silence to actually do so, but that was beside the point.

She'd been gradually eased back into work, not having realised just how bloody exhausted she was going to be. She wondered how much of it was because she'd been sitting around for six weeks as opposed to being a result of the operation itself, but she supposed it didn't really matter. Either way, she'd suffered the crushing realisation that she wasn't Superwoman after all.

The lack of energy was offset only by the overpowering, overwhelming boredom. Since she'd been on reduced duties, she'd felt her brain going to mush, and she knew that'd take much longer to overcome than physical tiredness. She'd been playing it down at work, showing Chief Superintendent Derek Arnold that she was perfectly capable of taking on bigger, beefier work. So far, though, there hadn't been anything particularly beefy to take on.

Mark and the boys had been wonderful. Mark had told his clients he'd be working shorter hours and taking some time off, and he'd been good to his word. She couldn't grumble about any of that; she just wished she'd never had to have the operation in the first place.

She and Mark had only ever wanted two children, and there'd been no question of having a third, but she couldn't deny it felt like a violation to have that choice taken away from her. It was something she couldn't put into words, which was the main reason she hadn't brought it up with Mark. She'd gone down her usual road of pretending everything was fine. Often, that was easier than bringing up issues or concerns. After all, what was the point? It wasn't going to change the material facts of the situation.

She selected a batch of emails she wasn't interested in and shouldn't have been sent anyway, and deleted them. The vast majority of stuff that got sent to her was completely pointless. She often wondered how many work hours were lost in police stations across the country because of needless emails. Someone had to sit down and write the things in the first place, then countless people had to open them, realise they were either nonsense or had been sent to the wrong person, then delete them. Even rounded down to five minutes a day, multiplied by however many police officers there were, spread across the year, would surely add up to enough money to at least fix the sodding coffee machine. Or, at the very least, they could avoid having to sell off police land to the private school next door.

By the time Caroline had reduced the number of unread emails in her inbox from 196 to 181, there was a knock on her door.

'Come in,' she called, watching as the door opened and Detective Sergeant Dexter Antoine poked his head round the door.

'Morning,' he said. 'How you feeling?'

'Morning, Dex. Depends who's asking.'

'A dead body.'

Caroline cocked her head slightly. 'Well, well. Medical science never ceases to amaze me. What do we know about our talking corpse?'

'Not a huge amount. Family out for a morning walk down near Harringworth Viaduct found him. Middle-aged guy in running gear, sitting up inside one of the arches.'

'Heart attack?'

'Doesn't look like it. Trauma to the head. Frozen solid, apparently. No idea how long he's been there.'

'At least fifteen minutes, judging by the weather out there this morning.'

Dexter chuckled. 'I don't fancy it much either. I presume it'll be going up to EMSOU, but thought I should let you know, anyway.'

It was normal for major crimes to be taken on by the East Midlands Special Operations Unit, but this was far from canon, and Caroline's background as a DCI with the Metropolitan Police before coming to Rutland meant she was always keen to take on cases for herself.

'Actually, isn't Harringworth in Northants?' she asked.

'The village is. Most of the viaduct is, too, but the northern part's in Rutland. Guess where our man is.'

'Typical. How far in?'

'Barely two hundred and fifty metres inside the county, believe it or not.'

'How inconsiderate.'

'I know. Still, it makes it even more fun to drag the EMSOU boys down from Derby or Nottingham for it, eh?'

Caroline thought for a moment. 'Actually, no. Don't do that.'

3

'Are you going to keep giving me the side-eye the whole way there?' Caroline asked as she turned off the A47 at Glaston and headed towards Seaton.

'I'm not,' Dexter replied.

'You are. I can see you. Don't worry, you're not going to catch me nodding off or blacking out. I'm perfectly capable of carrying on. If only you knew the hoops I had to jump through just to get into the office again.'

'And I know you'd find a way to jump through them, regardless.'

'I'm fine, Dex. I've had the exact amount of time off the doctor suggested, and I'm back at work with the blessing of my superior officers, who, I might just mention, one should always listen to.'

Dexter raised his hands as if to surrender. 'Alright. You're the boss.'

A few minutes later, Caroline's car came to a stop on the B672, a hundred yards or so short of the viaduct. The whole road had been closed, with an outer cordon formed to keep people away from the crime scene.

Caroline and Dexter got out of the car, feeling the bitter chill hit them the moment they did. Neither of them wanted to spend any longer out there than they had to. They showed their ID cards to PC Vickie Hughes, the officer manning the entry point, and asked her what she knew.

'Male, probably late forties to early fifties. Clearly been out for a run, as he's got all the gear on. Lycra shorts and all that. God knows how long he's been out here, but he's like a bloody Linford Christie ice lolly.'

'You had a lick?' Dexter asked, smiling.

'Course. Had to check the flavour. Rude not to.'

'Any signs of decomposition?' Caroline asked.

'Not much, to be honest. I'm no expert, but I'd say he's probably only been there overnight. Plenty of people come and walk their dogs round here, so they would have found him earlier otherwise.'

Caroline and Dexter stayed outside the inner cordon, the area that had to be kept forensically secure. Right from the start of any investigation, one of the main focuses had to be on ensuring they didn't cause any potential problems further down the line. It had been known for defence briefs to get their clients off a charge based on the same officers having attended the crime scene and later arrested the defendant. When the police then stood up in court to claim forensic accuracy, the case would fall apart over the possibility of cross-contamination.

'What sort of build?' Caroline asked.

'Runner's build. You know the sort. Slim. Wouldn't have lasted five minutes out here with the temperatures the way they've been. If it weren't for the blood, I'd have said it looks like he's sat down for a rest and frozen to death.'

They got as close as they could, watching as the body was moved to allow them sight of the back of the victim's head, which was caked with dried blood.

'Not much on the wall of the arch, is there?' Dexter asked.

'No, I was going to say,' PC Hughes replied. 'You'd expect to see a lot more, particularly with a head wound. There's not much on the ground, either.'

Another car arrived at the cordon. Dr David Duncan, the pathologist, spotted Caroline and walked towards them. 'Beautiful morning for it, isn't it?' he said, his smooth voice alone raising the temperature a couple of degrees.

'Not for him, it isn't,' Caroline said, nodding her head in the direction of the arch under the viaduct.

Dr Duncan smiled, the grey bristles of his beard moving as he did so. 'Well, we can't please them all, can we? Still, he's our client today, so I'd better go and make myself look presentable.'

Caroline and Dexter went and sat back in the car,

Caroline switching the engine back on to circulate some heat.

'I don't think we should hang around any longer than we need to,' Caroline said, rubbing her hands to try and keep warm. 'But if he's been killed then put in that position, we're going to need to get the whole area searched. I don't envy the poor buggers who'll have to do that. Just make sure they wrap up warm, at least.'

Caroline's phone rang, so she pressed to answer it through her car stereo. It was DC Sara Henshaw.

'Guv, are you still down at Seaton?'

'Ish. Middle of bloody nowhere, to be more precise. What's up?'

'We've just had a misper passed to us,' Sara said.

Dexter and Caroline looked at each other. A missing person reported on the same morning as a body was discovered didn't tend to be a coincidence.

'Go on,' Caroline said.

'A woman called Sandra Forbes filed the report. Says her husband, Martin Forbes, has been missing since last night, when he went out for a run. Last seen leaving his house on the edge of Seaton.'

'Let me guess the next bit. Late forties or early fifties, slim build, dressed in running gear?'

'Got it in one. Not a bad start to the morning, eh?'

'Not a bad start at all. Can you text the details over to me, please? We'll wait for Dr Duncan to do his bit, then we'll pop in and see Mrs Forbes on the way back.'

'Will do.'

'Cheers, Sara.'

Caroline ended the call and turned to Dexter. 'There we are,' she said. 'Now what was all that worry about easing me back in gently?'

4

A short while later, Caroline and Dexter stood at the edge of the inner cordon and watched as Dr Duncan carried out his examination. They didn't know anybody — apart, perhaps, from Dr Duncan — who particularly wanted to look at dead bodies close-up.

One of the underlying principles of forensic evidence was that of contact. When Locard said that every contact left a trace, this became the foundation on which forensic evidence as a marker of guilt was based. It was incredibly unlikely that a murder suspect had the victim's blood on their clothing because a police officer had forgotten to wash his hands after attending to the victim, then accidentally or otherwise smeared it all over the suspect's jumper. But 'incredibly unlikely' still didn't cut it in a court of law whose threshold for conviction was guilt beyond all reasonable doubt. Anything which allowed a defence lawyer to introduce the slightest level of doubt in a jury could be catastrophic.

After he'd concluded his initial observations, Dr Duncan skipped back over to Caroline and Dexter, looking more like a man who'd just proudly completed a particularly challenging jigsaw puzzle than someone who'd spent the last few minutes poking a dead body.

'Very interesting!' he said, beaming. 'This one'll keep you busy.'

'Go on. How bad is it?' Caroline asked.

'Well, he's dead,' Dr Duncan replied. 'So pretty bad, from his perspective. In terms of the cause of death, there's a pretty clear blow to the skull, towards the back but slightly towards his left-hand side. Impossible to say just yet whether he was facing the person who did it, but if he was I'd put money on them being right-handed. The opposite, if they were behind him.'

'He's fallen backwards against the wall, though, so does that mean he was facing them?' Dexter asked.

'Ah, no. See, this is where things get interesting. There's blood matting in his hair, but next to nothing on the brickwork he's propped up against. Certainly nowhere near the amount we'd expect to see if he ended up there immediately after the blunt trauma. Having said that, there are also signs of strangulation. There's petechial haemorrhaging in the eyes, for instance. So it's entirely possible the blow happened earlier but didn't kill him, and he was then strangled. We won't be able to say for certain until we've got him on the table. But there really isn't anything in the initial indications that suggest he put up a fight. No skin under the fingernails, no scratching. I did notice something suspicious, though.'

'Go on,' Caroline said.

'After death the heart stops beating, and the blood descends according to gravity. If you die on your back, for example, you end up with some lovely purple bruising all over the back of your body. Now, when we look at our chap here, we see the vast majority appears on the backs of his legs, but there are signs of blood pooling on his left-hand side. Small, but noticeable. It seems to indicate to me he either died on his left-hand side or was laid on it shortly after, and was then moved into this sitting position.'

'How long after are we talking?' Caroline asked.

'Difficult to say. Livor mortis can start in as little as twenty minutes, particularly in temperatures such as these. It might also mean the pooling on his left-hand side is more noticeable as a result. I wouldn't like to hazard a guess, but considering the ambient temperatures there's a decent chance he was moved within an hour of dying.'

Caroline nodded, trying to organise this information in her own mind. 'So can we determine how long he's been dead?'

Dr Duncan smiled. 'I wondered how long it'd take before you asked me that. The million dollar question, eh? Well, the huge caveat here is the conditions. Temperatures were sub-zero overnight and still are. We had icy winds through the night, too. All that will have sped up the cooling of the body, but rectal temperatures are usually pretty accurate, even if he is sitting on frozen ground.'

'Rather you than me,' Dexter remarked.

'To be honest, it's nice to have somewhere warm to pop your hands for a few moments. In the case of our customer over here, rigor mortis is heavily apparent. We'd usually expect to see that level of onset over the first twelve hours or more, but again, look at the conditions. If you chucked a leg of lamb in the freezer you'd expect it to stiffen up pretty quickly, and human meat's no different. It's likely we've got some freezing of the bodily fluids and fat tissues adding to the stiffness. Not that there's much fat on him. Looks like he was in pretty good shape.'

'Would that have made a big difference?' Caroline asked.

Dr Duncan shrugged. 'Difficult to say. Not as much fat tissue to freeze, but he'd certainly cool down much quicker. Out here, I imagine rigor mortis would've been sped up somewhat.'

'So are we talking overnight?'

'It probably won't surprise you that I wouldn't want to put a specific time on it, but I'd probably be looking somewhere around there. Even from a non-scientific point of view, he'd have been spotted long before now if he'd been there during the day yesterday. The rectal temperature seems to indicate somewhere in the early part of the night, but I wouldn't want to offer anything more specific just yet. Sorry.'

'No. No, that's fine. Thanks. Very helpful.'

Caroline and Dexter headed back towards the car, the bitter air cutting in through their clothes as they walked.

'Got to say, I'm looking forward to a warm cuppa and a biscuit at Mrs Forbes's house,' Dexter remarked.

'All that talk of rectal fingering got you peckish, has it?'

Dexter chuckled. 'Something like that.'

'Better hope that's not her husband over there, then, hadn't we?' Caroline replied. 'Otherwise I'm not sure PG Tips and a tin of Fox's will be the first thoughts on her mind.'

5

Sandra Forbes's house was an impressive farmhouse-style building on the far western edge of Seaton, bordered by a decent amount of open land. Caroline hadn't been measuring the distance, but it seemed like a fair old run from here to the viaduct, especially in this weather.

With the gate to the house closed, Caroline bumped her Volvo up onto the kerb and came to a stop at the end of the drive. 'Have to be careful how we handle this,' she said. 'Probably best we stick to the facts until we can get a positive ID, even though I think we both know which way this is going to go.'

Dexter smiled. 'What, you don't think there might be two slim middle-aged runners from Seaton who went out for a run last night and didn't come home?'

'I'm always one for keeping an open mind, Dex, but even I have my limits. Come on.'

As Sandra Forbes opened the door, she seemed to

clock immediately they were police officers, and her demeanour changed.

'Oh no. Oh no.'

'Mrs Forbes? I'm Detective Inspector Caroline Hills, and this is my colleague Detective Sergeant Dexter Antoine. I believe you made a call to the police about your husband?'

'Yes. Yes I did. You've found him, haven't you? What's happened?'

'Is it okay if we come in?' Caroline replied. They couldn't be too cautious when it came to telling people their loved ones had died, especially when they were yet to confirm for definite that this was the case.

The house was tastefully decorated — a lot of light-coloured wood and large windows — and Caroline felt almost out of place delivering such bad news in these positive and airy surroundings.

'Please. Please, can you just tell me what's happened. Please don't keep me waiting like this,' Sandra said as they reached the living room.

'We don't yet know what's happened,' Caroline said. 'A body has been discovered not far from Seaton, but we don't know for certain that it's Martin.'

Sandra's face dropped, and Caroline could almost see her soul disappear from her body as she registered this. 'What... what happened?'

'I think it's probably best that we confirm a few details first, if that's okay? We don't want to cause any undue distress if there's any chance the body isn't Martin.'

Sandra nodded slowly. 'Okay.'

'When did you last see Martin?'

'Uh, last night. About half six. He gets home from work about quarter-to, eats, then goes out for a run.'

'And what was he wearing?'

'I told them all this on the phone. A blue running top with reflective bits on it, black shorts, running shoes. He usually carries a small torch, too. The roads aren't that well lit round here.'

'Would he wear shorts even at this time of year?' Dexter asked.

'Yes. All the time. He comes home drenched in sweat whatever the weather.'

'And what time does he usually get home?' Caroline asked.

'Well, that depends. He's got a five kilometre route that goes out the other side of the village, round the back of the salvage yard and back in again. Then there's a ten kilometre one that goes up to Glaston, across to Morcott and back round. And more often than not he'll stop off at the George and Dragon on the way home.'

'Okay. So how long are we talking?'

'Oh, I don't know. If he does his short route then half an hour, maybe a bit more. If he does the full route and stops at the pub, who knows? I'm usually in bed by then.'

'And what time did you go to bed last night?'

'I really don't know. About eight, I think. I had a migraine coming on, and I realised he'd probably stopped off at the pub, so I left a note on the kitchen table. It happens quite a lot. He usually sleeps in the spare room so he doesn't disturb me.'

'I see. So you wouldn't necessarily have noticed he wasn't home until the next morning?'

'No, that's right. I got up this morning and thought he'd left for work early, but the door to the spare room was still open and the bed was perfectly made. He never leaves it like that, so I knew he hadn't slept in it.'

'So what did you do then?'

'I called him, but his phone was still on the side in the dining room, so I knew he hadn't come back after his run. He always leaves it there when he goes out running. He's got one of those fancy fitness watch things that tracks his times, heart rate and all that, then puts it all on his phone when he gets home. That's when I started to get worried, so I went out for a drive round his usual routes in case he'd been hit by a car or something, but I couldn't see him. So I phoned the police.'

'Okay. Thank you. Of course, we'll need to do a formal identification, but the description you've given us does match that of the body that was discovered this morning. It might be sensible to prepare yourself for the likelihood that the body is Martin.'

Sandra Forbes seemed to freeze in her seat, staring off into space. 'What... How?' she finally croaked.

'We're not sure yet, but we think he was hit round the head. It's possible that was what caused his death, but we'll have to wait for the post-mortem to confirm that.'

Sandra's eyes didn't leave the wall on the other side of the room. 'But it's so cold out there. It's freezing.'

Caroline nodded slowly. 'It's possible the cold might have played some part, particularly if Martin lost consciousness after the blow to the head. But as I say, we'll know soon what happened.'

'I can't... I can't identify him. I... I can't.'

'It's okay. If you don't feel comfortable with a physical identification, there are plenty of other ways we can do it. We can have an officer take Martin's hairbrush or toothbrush and we can match DNA from there.'

'But he... he needs it.'

Caroline and Dexter exchanged a look, a silent agreement between them that this conversation was going to require more specialist intervention.

6

They left Sandra Forbes in the capable hands of a trained Family Liaison Officer and uniformed constables, who would be able to carry out the administrative work of seizing Martin's hairbrush and toothbrush as evidence, as well as sensitively searching the home for anything else which might prove useful.

Having been shown photographs of Martin and compared those to the body found under Welland Viaduct, they were in no doubt that the body was his, and in their eyes a DNA match would be a mere formality. As a result, they'd informed Sandra that the body was overwhelmingly likely to be that of her husband.

As far as Caroline was concerned, this was a murder case. The blow to the back of Martin Forbes's head was substantial, and wasn't something he could've inflicted on himself. When that was coupled with strangulation and the possibility that Martin had died elsewhere and been moved underneath the viaduct after his death, all signs pointed towards murder.

Before they left, they'd managed to ascertain that Sandra didn't know of any arguments or enemies, or anyone who might want Martin dead. By all accounts he'd been a man who largely kept himself to himself, and wasn't the sort of person to fall out with people unnecessarily.

They'd established that Martin was the owner of a graphic design company based in Uppingham, and knew that by now the working day would've started in earnest, the rest of the employees naturally wondering where their boss had got to. In any case, their focus now turned to looking for suspects, motives and evidence, and it was clear they weren't going to get much more out of Sandra Forbes at the moment.

A little under ten minutes after leaving the Forbes house, they arrived outside the premises of Allure Design, the company Martin owned and ran, on the outskirts of Uppingham. Caroline pressed the buzzer on the outside of the door, and a few seconds later a voice answered.

'Hello?'

'Hello, Detective Inspector Hills and Detective Sergeant Antoine from Rutland Police. Can we come in, please?'

'Erm, well, I'm not sure. The boss isn't in and I don't want to…'

'No-one's in trouble,' Caroline said. 'We just have something we need to speak to you about.'

There was a short click, then a buzz as the door unlocked and Dexter pulled it open, before they both stepped inside. A thirty-something woman greeted them a few moments later.

'Sorry. Bit of a weird morning,' she said. 'I'm Monique. Operations and Finance Manager. How can I help?'

'Is there somewhere we can sit down?'

Monique took them through into what appeared to be a break room, and led them over to a seating area, which consisted of a dozen or so quarter-egg shaped chairs around a shocking pink and ridiculously shaggy circular rug.

'Wow. It's… bright in here.'

'Thanks! It was designed to spark impulsivity and engage the creative side of the mind.'

'Oh. It was designed?' Caroline asked.

'Yes,' Monique said, sitting down in a bright orange quarter-egg. 'By me.'

'Ah. Well, like I say, it's very… It's lovely.'

'Thank you. So, how can I help?'

'You mentioned your boss isn't here. I understand that's Martin Forbes, is that right?'

'Yes, dear old Martin. I mean, he's not *that* old, but most people here are under forty, so he gets that little sobriquet *de facto*.'

'Mmmm. Okay. When did you last see Martin?'

'Well, that would've been yesterday. It's usually one of

the two of us that locks up. I had to leave early last night, so I left Martin to it.'

'What time was this?'

'A minute or two after five. I had to dash. Why? Is there a problem?'

'I'm sorry to have to say that a body has been found, and that we believe it to be the body of Martin Forbes.'

'Oh. Oh my. Are you sure?'

'As certain as we can be, yes.'

'Oh my.' Monique made the sign of the cross. '*Requiescat in pace.*'

'Are you religious?' Caroline asked.

'No. Classically trained.'

'As what?'

Dexter gave Caroline a look. Fortunately, Monique seemed to have drifted off into a world of her own.

'What happened to him?' she asked. 'I mean, he's always so fit and healthy. He runs every day.'

'We're not certain yet, but we're currently investigating it as murder.'

'Murder? Oh my.'

'Yes. We're sorry to have to ask you this, but had Martin had any strong disagreements with anyone recently? Did he have any enemies or perhaps anyone who'd been upset in business?'

Monique looked at Caroline as if she'd just bent over and passed wind. 'No, of course not. Martin didn't make enemies. I mean, he was strong-minded. He knew what he wanted. He was a *nulla tenaci invia est via* sort of chap, if you know what I mean.'

'I don't.'

'It means "For the tenacious, no road is impassable". You need to be pretty strong-willed in this business, but not on a level which would make anyone want to… Well, you know.'

'Yes. Did his tenacity tend to upset people, then?'

'Well, no. Not exactly.'

'Not exactly?'

'He was never mean or nasty. He's a… I think at heart he was a good person. He always strove for better. I mean, the company's motto is quite literally "*Non progredi est regredi.*" What more could you ask for?'

'A translation?'

'It means "To not go forward is to go backward". Wise words in business.'

'Did he come up with that motto?' Caroline asked, noticing Dexter trying not to smile.

Monique thought for a moment. 'No, I think I did actually.'

Caroline faked a reaction of impressed surprise. 'I see. So no workplace disagreements or fallings out at all?'

Monique opened her mouth to reply, but then stopped.

'Monique?'

'Well, these things happen in the workplace don't they?'

'That's what we're hoping to find out. What's the specific example you have in mind?'

'Well, there was one recently. It wasn't anything major. And I don't want to drop anyone in it unnecessarily.'

'In my experience, you never know what information might prove to be pertinent. It's always best we know everything and filter it at this end, believe me.'

Monique swallowed. 'Okay. Well, one of our designers, Amie Tanner, went into Martin's office at the back end of last week. Thursday or Friday, I think it was. I didn't catch how the conversation started, but I began to hear raised voices. I mean, on the surface of things, it was just a disagreement over a project she was working on. But it didn't quite make any sense.'

'How do you mean?' Caroline asked.

'Well, it was clear there was something else under the surface. To me, it seemed like they'd fallen out over something else, and it was all bubbling to a head over this silly work thing instead.'

'I see. Amie Tanner, is she in today?'

'No, she's working from home today. She's got two young girls and her husband works shifts, so she tries to work from home at half term, as much as possible.'

'Do you have her address?'

'Not off the top of my head, but I can find it. It'll be on the system.'

'Thank you. That'd be much appreciated. Oh, speaking of which, we'll need to speak to whoever looks after your computer systems. Our IT forensics people will need to take a look.'

'Oh. Well, that'd be Tom. But he's not in today. He's

due back tomorrow, I think. I can get his number, if that helps?'

'Yes please. That'd be great if it's not too much trouble.'

'Of course! *Nil volentibus arduum.*'

Caroline smiled and watched as Monique left the room.

'Bloody hell, is *anyone* in work today?' Caroline asked.

'These designer types,' Dexter replied. 'Probably busy gazing out of windows. Still, obviously does the job. Looks great in here, doesn't it?'

'Does it? And what's with all the Latin phrases? It's like interviewing Julius bloody Caesar.'

'I think the term is "Quidquid latine dictum sit, altum videtur",' Dexter said.

'Not you as well,' Caroline replied, sighing. 'Go on, then. What does that one mean?'

'"Anything said in Latin sounds profound."'

7

Caroline stood in front of her team, ready to lead the first briefing on what would henceforth be known as Operation Cruickshank, the name chosen at random by the police computer.

Each time she chose to take on a major case, she had conflicted emotions. There was the natural excitement and adrenaline rush of chasing a killer and getting justice for a family, but at the same time she felt a rising panic at the thought of having to carry out such a huge investigation with a team so limited by numbers.

They were, as with any police force, heavily reliant on their uniformed colleagues, but major investigations tended to be carried out by huge teams at a regional level. So far, Caroline had managed to exploit the fact that this was merely tradition and recommended practice, and wasn't set in stone.

She knew, though, that if she didn't continue to get

results despite the odds being stacked against her, she'd face impossible pressure to hand all future cases over to EMSOU, the East Midlands Special Operations Unit.

It wasn't just her ego that would take a hit. It'd be a huge blow to her colleagues in Rutland CID, who continued to blow her away with their commitment and enthusiasm. She'd developed a loyal right-hand man in DS Dexter Antoine, and had come to regard him as a friend. Likewise, Detective Constables Sara Henshaw and Aidan Chilcott continued to go above and beyond the call of duty, and had been instrumental in solving two huge cases in the past year.

'Okay, welcome to the first morning briefing on Operation Cruickshank, the investigation into the murder of Martin Forbes, whose body was found below Welland Viaduct. Martin was a businessman from Seaton who ran a design agency in Uppingham. He was married, to Sandra, and they have two sons, who are currently away at university. Martin was known to be a keen runner, and he'd been out running on Monday night, when it's believed he was murdered. We know from speaking with his wife he owned and wore a fitness watch, which we've so far been unable to recover.'

'Potential mugging gone wrong?' Aidan asked.

'Unlikely. Who mugs a runner? It's not like they're carrying valuables. And no-one's that desperate for a Fitbit. The cause of death is yet to be determined, but first inspection of the body in situ revealed trauma to the back of the head, as well as signs of strangulation, probably with a forearm. Again, more detail to come, but there's a good chance his killer struck him then strangled him in a headlock. Crucially, there's a very limited amount of blood at the scene, which is unusual with a head wound like this. This leads us onto the possibility that Martin was killed elsewhere, then transported to the viaduct, but that in itself is confusing because we know Martin's running route passed by the exact spot where he was found. His body wasn't visible from the road, and was only discovered when a family out walking found him early this morning. Rather annoyingly, there was quite a bit of rainfall yesterday evening, before the temperature dropped. That means crucial evidence — like blood — is likely to have been washed away.'

'Not from the location where his body was found, though,' Dexter added.

'Indeed. Even with the rainfall we had, there's no way it would've washed the walls of the arches free of blood. There's still a lot we don't know at this stage, but we visited his business premises and spoke to his Operations and Finance Manager, a woman called Monique Dupont. She mentioned that he was generally a fairly likeable chap, but that he'd recently had an argument in the office with a woman called Amie Tanner, one of their designers. It's probably nothing, but we're following it up anyway. Sara, did you have any luck researching Allure Design? Was Martin the sole director?'

Sara Henshaw shook her head. 'No, his wife is also

listed. As I understand it, the company remains active and passes to her.'

'Alright. Interesting. Pretty much what I expected, though, and doesn't necessarily mean anything. We've also managed to get hold of Allure's IT manager, Tom Mackintosh, but he's away in Scotland on holiday. He's due back late tonight, so he's going to help us access the company's emails and systems tomorrow. It's a tenuous lead at best, so it didn't seem worth us barging in and seizing the lot, especially as the company's still operating.

'Amie Tanner's currently working from home as she's got two kids, but her husband's got the day off today, so she's agreed to come in for a voluntary interview. Didn't want us round there with the kids about, which is fine by me. Saves us going out in this weather again. Dex and I will speak to her when she arrives. In the meantime, we need to look further into Martin. There's a team searching his home as we speak, and another looking for evidence at and near the scene. Fingers crossed the rain was kind to us. Sara, can I leave you in charge of looking into Martin? And Aidan, can you see if there are any houses, business premises or anything anywhere on Martin Forbes's running route which might have CCTV? I think our best bet's likely to be the George and Dragon pub in Seaton, but it'd be handy to do a walk round checking residentials as well as anything else we've missed on the route.'

'Yep, got it,' Aidan said. 'Anything else?'

'Just one thing,' Caroline replied. 'Take your woolly hat.'

8

The call came in from the front desk to let Caroline know Amie Tanner had arrived for her voluntary interview. It'd be a good opportunity to find out more about Martin and the sort of person he was. Although they didn't yet have much to go on, it was often the case that you could get two very different impressions of the same person by speaking to two different acquaintances. Caroline's maxim was *Know the victim*, and that had proven far more useful to her than any other tip or strategy she'd picked up in her years of policing. In the overwhelming majority of cases, people were killed because of who they were or what they'd done. If you managed to get to the bottom of who the victim was and what they'd been up to, you were — more often than not — mere inches from identifying their killer.

Caroline and Dexter made their way down to the interview room, where Amie Tanner was waiting for them. She seemed quiet — calm, but confident — and gave a slight smile from the side of her mouth as they entered the room.

'Amie?' Caroline asked.

'Yes. Hi.'

'I'm Detective Inspector Caroline Hills. This is my colleague, Detective Sergeant Dexter Antoine. Thank you for coming in to see us today. Do you live locally?'

'Market Overton.'

Caroline nodded. Amie was clearly a woman of few words. 'Can we get you a drink or anything?'

'No, I'm fine thanks.'

'Okay. Shall we get started, then?'

Amie nodded.

'So you know by now that Martin Forbes was found dead this morning. He was your boss, is that correct?'

'Yes.'

'And what was he like? As a person, I mean.'

Amie sighed. 'Well, he was alright. Friendly, I guess.'

Caroline got the distinct impression Amie would rather be anywhere else than here. 'Have you been working there long?' she asked.

'Yeah, years.'

'And have you always got along well with him?'

'Pretty much.'

'Pretty much?' Caroline asked, starting to get more than a little annoyed with Amie's brevity. She understood this wasn't the most natural way to spend one's day, but she'd expected a little more cooperation. On the contrary,

Amie's terseness was beginning to strike Caroline as a little suspicious.

Almost as if she'd clocked on to this, Amie shifted in her chair and began to speak. 'Well, we had a bit of a disagreement last week. I'm guessing that's why you've asked me to come in here. And why you're asking about how we got on.'

Caroline really didn't know how to process Amie. Although she didn't like to generalise or put people in boxes, it was generally true to say there were certain "types" which applied to most people she came across in the job. But none of them seemed to quite fit when it came to Amie Tanner. Her paucity with words might've left Caroline with the impression Amie was shy, but there was a definite confidence about her. It wasn't coldness, either. Try as she might, she couldn't quite put her finger on it.

'What was the disagreement about?' Caroline asked.

'Just a work project,' Amie said, sighing and easing back into her chair. 'I thought we were going in the wrong direction with it. Martin disagreed.'

'I see. Did you fall out often?'

'No, not really. It's just the way it goes sometimes. Clients hire us to do the work, pay through the nose for our expertise, then tell us they think we're doing it wrong and try to tell us a different way of doing things.'

'And Martin backed them up?'

Amie shrugged. 'He's all about following the money. I can see his point — it's a business. But it's a design agency too, and if we put out crap designs to please one client, we'll easily do ourselves out of another ten.'

'Makes sense to me. Was it quite a noisy disagreement, then?'

'Probably. It's not the first time, so I imagine a few frustrations boiled over.' Amie looked at them, seemingly registering that Caroline and Dexter knew a little more than they were letting on. 'I mean, I got a few funny looks from the others when I came out of his office, so I'm guessing most people probably overheard it and would've said it was loud.'

Caroline deliberately chose not to address her thinly-veiled attempt to find out who'd been talking. 'What were the other disagreements usually over? Work, or something else?'

'Yes, work,' Amie replied, looking at her as if she'd just asked if she were a human or a frog. 'That's how it is at design agencies. You've got creative people at one end, business people at the other and people like me in the middle, trying to balance it all and keep everyone happy.'

'Must be quite an interesting work environment,' Caroline said, looking at Dexter. 'I know if DS Antoine here argued with me and told me I was doing things wrong, I'd have him strung up.'

Dexter tried to keep a straight face. They both knew the professional structure at Rutland CID was far removed from most other police forces, never mind any other organisation.

'Like I say,' Amie replied, 'design agencies are a whole different world of their own.'

'So did lots of other people tend to have arguments with Martin?'

Amie gave a slight shrug. 'I dunno, really. Some probably did. You know what it's like. There are those who're happy to put their views forward, and others who think the same thing but prefer to moan behind people's backs. At least no-one can call me duplicitous or two-faced.'

Caroline could think of another few words she was sure no-one would use to describe Amie.

'Anyway, it's not out-and-out arguments you want to be looking into,' Amie continued.

'How do you mean?'

She sighed. 'Between you and me, Martin liked to think of himself as a bit of a ladies' man.'

'I see. And is that something you had personal experience of?'

'Absolutely not. No chance. But it doesn't mean I didn't know what was going on.'

'And what was going on, Amie?' Caroline asked, starting to become sick of her riddles and vague comments.

Amie looked at her. 'If you want to know what's been going on, it's Monique you want to talk to. Not me.'

'Oh? Is there something we should know?'

Amie let out a small *harumph*, a semi-sarcastic attempt at laughter, which sounded more like an overweight child landing on a bouncy castle. 'Well, let's just say she has a far more intimate knowledge of Martin than I ever would.'

In her career as a detective, she'd come across many cases where people had killed over petty arguments or what might have appeared to be minor disagreements. But those had tended to either involve snap reactions or highly unstable people. Amie was odd — there was no doubt about that — but she appeared stable enough. It seemed extremely unlikely that she'd kill someone in cold blood a few days after a professional disagreement over a work project. It didn't quite stack up. But then there were a lot of things which were already failing to stack up when it came to this case. And — try as she might — Caroline couldn't shake the feeling that there was something deeply unsettling about Amie Tanner.

9

Aidan and Sara pulled up outside the George & Dragon pub in Seaton, and Aidan glanced at his watch.

'I'll pop in and see what they've got on their CCTV. Do you want to have a wander and see if there're any residential cameras?'

'I can't imagine it'll take long,' Sara replied. 'Population of two hundred people in the whole village, apparently. I doubt if there are thirty buildings on his entire running route. Might be better if we do it all together. At least that way we won't miss anything.'

Aidan furrowed his brow and looked at her. 'You do know you're not allowed to drink on duty, don't you, Detective Constable Henshaw? We can't have you sinking double gin and tonics all afternoon if that's your idea.'

Sara laughed and shook her head as Aidan's face broke into a smirk. 'You're a dick, Aidan.'

'And that's another thing you need to learn, Detective

Constable,' Aidan said, getting out of the car. 'If you're going to insult your fellow officers, put some effort in and at least make it better than what my last customer called me.'

'Now you've got my attention,' Sara replied. 'Mind if I take a few guesses?'

'Only if you're willing to write it up in your PCB.'

'On second thoughts, I'm not sure the paperwork appeals. I'll just stick to insulting you in my head.'

Sara opened the front door of the George & Dragon and they stepped inside. She was pretty sure she'd never been in here before, but she had a feeling she'd be back. It was a cosy blend of traditional and modern, with a clear focus on food and wine — two things Sara was always more than happy to see.

It was a quiet afternoon, but they were quickly greeted by the owner, who poured them each a complimentary orange juice.

'I'm guessing this is about the body down by the viaduct?' he asked, handing over the drinks.

'It is, yeah,' Aidan replied. 'Do you know much about it?'

The man shook his head. 'Not really. Only hearsay off the locals. Found hanging by a dog walker, wasn't he?'

'Not quite,' Aidan said, never ceasing to be amazed at how social media and the local rumour mill could distort facts so easily. 'Did you know him well?'

'The chap who died? No, don't think so. Not even sure who it was, to be honest. One of the locals said they saw police cars up the other end of the village this morning, so I presume he lived there.'

Aidan was almost impressed. The pub had barely been open a couple of hours, and he was certain the only car that had attended Sandra Forbes's house was Caroline's very much unmarked Volvo. Then again, people did seem to have an uncanny knack for spotting a plain-clothes police officer a mile off. He unlocked his phone and pulled up a photo of Martin. 'Do you recognise this chap at all?' he asked.

The man studied the photo for a few moments, looking as though he was ploughing the depths of his memory. 'Yeah, he's familiar. He's been in here before, I'm sure of it.'

'Is he a regular, would you say?'

'I wouldn't say so, no.'

'Has he been in recently?'

'Depends what you mean by recent, really. Is that the only photo you've got of him?'

'No, there's another one,' Aidan replied, swiping the screen on his phone and bringing up a recent picture of Martin and Sandra Forbes.

'Ah. Yes. It's been a while since he was in, I think, but I remember her alright.'

'The woman?' Aidan asked.

'Yeah. His wife, isn't it?'

'Yeah. Has she been in?'

'Week or so ago, I think. Maybe a bit more. She came in all nervous and flustered, looking round the pub. One of the bar staff asked if she was okay and she said she was looking for her husband. Once she'd seen he wasn't here, she left again.'

Aidan and Sara exchanged a glance. 'Is that something that happens a lot?' Aidan asked him.

'From time to time. I wouldn't say a lot, but you do sometimes get people trying to find their other half. Used to happen quite a bit back in the day, before mobile phones and all that. Alcoholics and big drinkers picking somewhere the missus wouldn't think to look for them. Much rarer now, of course.'

'Was that the only time this woman had been in?'

'Oh no, I'm pretty sure she's been in with him before. Not for a while, mind. Don't know them by name or anything. Why's that? Is he the chap they found dead?'

Aidan's first instinct was to try to change the subject, keen to ensure that the family's privacy was respected and that rumours didn't start about Sandra Forbes winching her husband up into a tree in front of a gaggle of dog walkers. Realistically, though, he knew people would form their own theories and conclusions no matter what he did.

Aidan cleared his throat. 'I don't suppose there's any chance we could have a quick look at your CCTV box, is there?'

10

As much as Caroline disliked darting backwards and forwards across the county numerous times a day, there was no substitute for seeing the whites of people's eyes. Phone calls didn't quite cut it in the same way. And while calling people in for interviews was certainly a lot easier, there was often a lot to be gained by speaking to them in their natural environment.

Aidan had called her to update her on what they'd discovered at the George & Dragon in Seaton, and it had certainly got more than a few cogs turning in her mind.

She parked a little further up the road from Allure Design's offices than she had previously, and walked the last few dozen yards.

As she got there, she noticed the heavy front door hadn't been fully closed. She thought about pressing the intercom button anyway, but decided against it. An open door was an open door.

She stepped inside and gently closed the door behind her. The office was quiet, as was to be expected considering the circumstances, but it was clear somebody was still here. A vaguely familiar whirring noise came from the far side of the building, and as Caroline stepped forward she noticed the light spilling out through the doorway into what had been Martin Forbes's office.

She reached the doorway and looked inside. Monique was on all fours with her back to Caroline, feeding sheets of paper into a large shredder.

Caroline knocked on the door with her knuckle, watching as Monique almost jumped clean out of her clothes.

'Sorry, hope I didn't frighten you.'

'Oh! No. No. How did you get in here?'

'Door's open,' Caroline replied, thumbing a gesture over her shoulder. 'What you doing?'

'Just some filing. Nothing important,' Monique answered, climbing to her feet and straightening out the creases in her black pencil skirt. It was clear from her body language that something wasn't quite right.

Caroline looked at the papers on the floor. 'Those are invoices, aren't they?'

'Old ones,' Monique replied, bending back down and scooping them up. 'No use having them cluttering up the place, is there?'

'This one's dated last month,' Caroline said, picking up an invoice and inspecting it.

'Yes, well, everything's digitised now, isn't it? It's all

dealt with, and we try to be as environmentally friendly as we can.'

'By feeding paper into an electric shredder?'

'It gets recycled. That can't happen if it's in a filing cabinet. Anyway, can I help you?'

Caroline looked around the office, enjoying the fact she'd taken Monique by surprise and put her on the back foot. It had crossed her mind that there'd been a distinct lack of Latin phraseology so far, too.

'I was hoping to ask you a couple of questions about your relationship with Martin Forbes,' she said, looking back at Monique. Now that she'd caught her on the hop, she felt like a predator going in for the kill. Monique had clearly been up to no good, and seemed far too keen to stop Caroline getting a closer look at any of the paperwork she'd been shredding.

'You've already asked me that,' Monique replied.

'Ah. No, I mean your other relationship.'

The response was subtle — a slight facial twitch — but Caroline had been looking for it, and it had made itself apparent.

'Sorry. I don't know what you mean. Now, I really must get on.'

'So you're telling me you weren't having a sexual relationship with Martin Forbes?' she asked, looking her dead in the eyes. It was clever wording from Caroline. She hadn't made an accusation, hadn't verbalised it as a statement, but had loaded the question with enough weight to make a guilty party aware of what she knew.

Monique swallowed, her fake eyelashes fluttering like plastic insects trying to take off. 'Uh, well, I don't know quite what you're insinuating, but—'

'It's a perfectly simple question,' Caroline replied.

Monique let out a sigh, the tension visibly easing from her body as she perched herself against the edge of Martin's desk and folded her arms. A defensive motion, Caroline noted.

'What do you already know?' Monique asked.

'I'll ask the questions, if that's okay. How long has it been going on?'

Monique shrugged. 'A while.'

'Months? Years?'

'Closer to the latter.'

Caroline nodded. A long-term affair. A classic example of a situation ready to explode, with deadly consequences. She'd need to ensure everything was recorded in an official statement from Monique, but she got the sense that now wasn't the time to approach that. At the very least, Monique was talking. 'Was it serious?' Caroline asked.

Monique made a noise that sounded like somebody deflating a beach ball. 'No. Of course not. It was just sex.'

'For years?'

'Not far off. I haven't exactly been keeping a diary.'

'Who else knew?'

'No-one, as far as I was aware. But clearly someone's figured it out and told you.'

Caroline ignored the thinly veiled request for names. 'Was Martin's wife aware?'

'I doubt it. Awareness has never really been her strong point. She's either brilliant at burying her head in the sand or she genuinely has no idea who she was married to.'

Caroline sensed there was something hidden beneath those final words. Could there have been more to Martin's vices than an extra-marital affair? 'What do you mean?' she asked.

'Nothing. It's fine.'

'It really isn't. If you have information which could lead to Martin's killer, why would you want to withhold it?'

Monique shuffled awkwardly. 'It won't lead to Martin's killer.'

'And how could you possibly know that?' Caroline asked, cocking her head.

'I think it's best I consult a lawyer before I say anything else,' Monique replied, her voice almost a whisper.

Caroline nodded. So this was how it was going to be. 'There's certainly a way we can speed that up, Monique. I'm afraid I'm left with very little alternative but to place you under arrest and bring you in for formal questioning.'

11

Later that day, Caroline was busily preparing for their initial interview with Monique Dupont. The discovery that Monique lived in nearby Harringworth made perfect sense. Martin hadn't been stopping at the pub in the evenings — he'd been running the mile and a half to Monique's house, spending a couple of hours with her, then running home again. It was a wonder he had any energy left.

CCTV footage from the George & Dragon showed Martin jogging past the pub on the night he died, heading east. With a crossroads just a few yards beyond the bounds of the cameras, it was conceivable he could have gone in any direction just moments later, but the working assumption had to be that he'd headed south towards Harringworth, before skirting left at Seaton Meadows and under the viaduct, where he'd been found.

After arresting Monique, Caroline had requested

uniformed backup to take their new suspect back to the station, as well as to assist in bagging and tagging evidence. Monique's work laptop, which had been discovered on Martin's desk, had been seized along with the invoices that had been destined for the shredder. The laptop would be analysed forensically, and it had been agreed that news of Monique's arrest would be kept quiet from the rest of Allure's staff until the following day, when they'd be able to fully access and make copies of the rest of the company's computer systems.

Sara knocked on Caroline's office door and stepped inside. 'I've been looking at those invoices you snapped photos of,' she said. 'I think we might have something.'

'Go on.'

'They all seem to be for the same company, DQK Consultancy. They're all pretty vague. "Services rendered", "consultancy services provided", that sort of thing. Only a few hundred quid here and there, but it all starts to add up pretty quickly. Anyway, I did a search at Companies House to see what I could find out about this company. Turns out there's only one director, by the name of Doris Knowles.'

'Okay. The name doesn't ring a bell, but I'm guessing by the look on your face it should.'

Sara smiled. 'Not necessarily. But the director's service address listed for Doris Knowles is familiar. It's Monique Dupont's home address.'

'Ah-ha. All innocent and above board, or has she been siphoning cash off to a housemate?'

'Neither. I had a hunch, so I did a bit more digging. Doris Knowles changed her name by deed poll a number of years ago. To Monique Dupont.'

Caroline let out an involuntary cackle. 'Seriously? Her real name is Doris? That's made my bloody day, that has. I can't wait to drop that one on her. So she's been raising fake invoices to Allure from her own company and using her position as Finance Manager to pay them? That's embezzlement, surely.'

'If we can prove they weren't authorised,' Sara replied.

'And the one person who could've testified to that was Martin Forbes. It's all starting to make sense now. Do we know how much she took in total?'

Sara shook her head. 'No idea. We'll know once the guys have been through the accounts software and the bank info, but even just from the invoices we managed to seize from the premises we're looking at thousands, if not tens of thousands.'

'Wow. What a mess. Brilliant work, Sara. Absolutely fantastic. Between you and me, I think I'm going to have a lot of fun in this interview.'

12

Caroline walked into the interview room feeling like the cat that got the cream. She sat down next to Dexter, opposite Monique and her solicitor, both of whom looked as though they'd rather be anywhere else.

'Okay Monique,' she said, starting the interview. 'Let's begin by recapping what you told me earlier today at your workplace, shall we? For the record, you told me that you'd been having a relationship with Martin Forbes for some time. To use your words, it was "just sex". Is that correct?'

Monique replied without looking up. 'No comment.'

'Right,' Caroline said, sighing. 'Now, I don't know if that's something you've got off the telly or if your solicitor told you to say that, but I'll give you credit and presume it's the latter. He may well have led you to believe that because you told me about the affair before you were arrested, it won't be admissible in court. First of all, that's not strictly correct. In fact, it would likely count heavily against you in court if you were shown to have retracted evidential statements which we can otherwise prove to be true.'

'Those last four words being the crucial ones,' the solicitor remarked.

'I don't think they'll be an issue,' Caroline replied, smiling and turning her attention back to Monique. 'Besides which, if you're as innocent as you make out, you have nothing to worry about, do you? Holding things back is only going to prolong the situation. So it was "just sex", was it?'

Monique looked briefly at her solicitor, and Caroline could see her confidence in him had started to fall. 'No comment,' she whispered.

'Okay. In that case, let's move on to something else. We can circle back round later. When I came back to the offices of Allure Design earlier today, I found you shredding some documents. Can you tell me what they were please?'

'No comment.'

'That's fine. We seized the rest of them anyway, plus the ones that had already been shredded. It's an impressive cross-cut shredder, but you'd be amazed at what our guys can do nowadays, especially if they've got an idea what they're looking for. I imagine that'll be more invoices, will it? That's what made up the rest of the pile.'

Monique chose not to answer.

'The invoices were all made out to a company called DQK Consultancy. Have you heard of them?'

She glanced at her solicitor again before answering, this time even less convincingly. 'No comment.'

'The sole director of DQK Consultancy is somebody called Doris Knowles. Does that name ring any bells?'

Caroline watched as Monique clenched her jaw. She could tell from the body language between her and her solicitor that she'd already disclosed the truth to him. They must have been well aware this was going to come out.

'Doris Knowles is you, isn't it?' she asked.

'I hated the name,' Monique answered, through gritted teeth. 'It was my grandmother's name. She died two weeks before I was born. I never even met the woman, and I already got saddled with a dead person's name. I wouldn't have minded if it was a *nice* name, but it's just so… *common.*'

Caroline raised her eyebrows. 'Well I'm sure your nan's jumping for joy up there at the way you chose to honour her memory.'

'Like I say, I never met her. There was nothing about my name that particularly appealed.'

'So you changed your name. To the rather… different… Monique Dupont.'

'Yes.'

'Why did you form DQK Consultancy in your old name then?'

Monique took a deep breath, then exhaled heavily. 'I don't know. I wanted a bit of distance.'

'And has DQK Consultancy ever functioned as an

actual business, or does it exist purely to embezzle funds from Allure Design?'

The solicitor cleared his throat. 'Detective Inspector, please take care with your choice of words.'

Caroline ignored him and looked at Monique. 'Monique?'

'Martin knew about it,' she said eventually. 'I raised invoices from DQK to Allure, then paid them through Allure's accounts.'

'Okay. Why?'

Monique shrugged. 'Why not?'

'You tell me. Tax dodge?'

'No. I've always paid my taxes in full.'

'So what was it then? Just stealing money for the fun of it?'

'I told you. Martin knew. You can't accuse me of stealing something from someone who knew about it and let it happen.'

'We've only got your word for that, haven't we? Martin, quite conveniently, happens to be dead. In any case, Sandra Forbes is also a director of Allure Design. Did she know you'd been embezzling funds?'

'Detective Inspector,' the solicitor grumbled.

'I don't want to answer that question,' Monique replied.

Caroline jotted some notes on the pad in front of her as she spoke. 'Okay. I'm sure your solicitor will make you aware of this if he hasn't already, but Martin Forbes having been an accessory to your act of fraud perpetrated against a company co-owned by his unknowing wife doesn't absolve you of any liability in that regard. Just so we're clear. But let's circle back round on this. Your relationship with Martin. Did that begin before or after you started this little scheme?'

Monique swallowed. 'After.'

Caroline and Dexter exchanged a brief glance. 'I see. And were you as keen on the idea as he was?' She watched as Monique tried desperately to hide her reaction, lost in the confusion as to what she should be willing to tell them. 'Did he coerce you into a sexual relationship in exchange for allowing the embezzlement to continue?'

Monique's jaw began to tremble as tears filled her eyes. Eventually, she closed them and nodded.

Caroline looked at Dexter again. They both knew what the implications were. If Martin Forbes had coerced Monique into regularly having sex with him, effectively in exchange for money, it shifted the power dynamic substantially. But it also gave her a prime motive for murder.

'Okay,' Caroline said, now acutely aware of her duty of care towards Monique. 'How do you feel? Are you happy to continue or would you like a few minutes?'

Monique shook her head and sniffed. 'No. It's fine. I want this all over with as quickly as possible.'

'Alright. In that case, I'm sorry to have to ask you this, but can you tell me where you were between six o'clock yesterday evening and nine o'clock this morning?'

'At my mum's in Corby, for most of it.'

'Most of it? Can you be a little more specific please?'

Monique sighed. 'Okay, well I left work at the usual time and went straight round there. I stayed overnight until I left for work this morning. So no, it's physically impossible for me to have killed Martin, if that's what you're asking.'

'We are going to need to verify that, Monique. I hope you understand.'

'Verify it all you like. I stayed over because my dad's in hospital. They had a break-in a few years back, and the guys beat my dad to a pulp. It made the papers and everything. He had a bleed on the brain. He's never been the same since. He gets seizures every now and then. Every few months, perhaps. Each time he does, he has to stay overnight in hospital for observation. Mum called me yesterday afternoon to say it'd happened again, so I stayed over with her. She's petrified to sleep in the house on her own after what happened. Especially when the whole reason dad's not there is because of the break-in.'

'I'm sorry to hear that,' Caroline said, mentally noting that it wouldn't be difficult to confirm all this from police reports and hospital records.

'And if you need proof,' Monique said, as if reading Caroline's mind, 'that won't be difficult either. They've done the place out like Fort Knox since that day. CCTV cameras, video doorbells, the lot. I was probably on more cameras and screens last night than Richard Osman.'

Caroline nodded. They'd have to access the footage as quickly as possible to verify her alibi, especially in light of the revelation that Monique had been a victim of sexual coercion. Caroline didn't like to use the word lightly, but there could be a strong argument for calling it rape by deception or fraud.

'Okay. We're going to need to check the footage and confirm everything at this end. We'll pull out all the stops to do that as quickly as we possibly can.'

'Will I have to wait here, or can I go?'

Caroline pursed her lips. They hadn't yet got any proof of what Monique was saying, and even if she could prove her whereabouts it didn't clear her of conspiracy or some level of involvement. 'We'll need you to hold on a little longer, if that's okay.'

Monique slowly nodded. 'Yeah. Yeah okay. Just… try and be quick. Please. I really want to see my dad.'

13

As much as she wanted to push forward, Caroline felt powerless. Officers had been despatched to Monique's mother's house in Corby and the security footage had proven that Monique wasn't their killer, having spent the whole night at her mother's.

More than anything, it had given them their first real glimpse into the sort of man Martin Forbes had been, and it hadn't exactly reduced the field of potential suspects. For now, though, it was a waiting game.

Caroline had been forced to put the brakes on the planned full forensic analysis of Allure Design's computer systems and accounts. Now that it would be merely speculative, she simply couldn't justify the expense on what were already extremely tight policing budgets. In any case, she'd decided to proceed with obtaining a backup of everything from their systems, just in case it was needed further down the line. If nothing else, it would ensure nothing was 'accidentally' lost or misplaced.

It was often the case that investigations relied on third parties cooperating quickly and effortlessly, and delays and roadblocks were, at times, unbearable. With Allure Design's IT manager, Tom Mackintosh, still being on holiday, there was very little they could do until he returned.

In the situation where they were pretty certain conclusive evidence was on the company's computer systems, a court order could allow them to seize the equipment, but that wasn't the route Caroline wanted to go down. A court order would take time to obtain, and it was likely it wouldn't arrive much before Tom Mackintosh did. Then there were the concerns that the business needed to keep running. As a limited company, Allure was a separate legal entity to Martin Forbes, and was now under the management of its sole director, Sandra Forbes. Caroline didn't know how long that would continue, as the impression she got was that Sandra didn't take much of an interest in the running of the company, but with salaries and livelihoods at stake, they needed to tread carefully.

In any case, their desire to search the IT systems was more speculative than anything else. Caroline didn't think for one minute they'd log on and find a stash of death threats or confession letters, but it would at least help them to build up a bigger picture and could potentially develop further leads. She was also keen to further explore the link between Martin and Monique, as well as the possibility that she hadn't been his only victim.

With Martin dead, Sandra at home and half the staff already off on holiday, the decision had been made to return tomorrow, with officers in attendance to make sure they obtained an accurate backup of the company's IT systems.

By the evening, Caroline's head was pounding. She'd done well in her convalescence and had made excellent progress, but sitting around doing very little had sapped her energy levels, both mentally and physically. She could see now why it had been recommended she return on reduced duties, but there was no way she was going to admit that to anyone.

She sat on the sofa as Mark cooked dinner, the smells beginning to waft through the house, making her hungry. One of the worst parts of recovering at home had been the tension that'd developed between them. They'd done their best to keep it from Archie and Josh, but that hadn't done them any favours in their own relationship. By the time the boys were in bed, Caroline was far too tired to get into any in-depth discussions.

Try as she might, she still couldn't come to terms with the way the operation had made her feel. Although she and Mark hadn't planned to have any more children, the fact that this decision had now been taken away from her was extraordinarily difficult to accept. Mark had predictably reminded her at every opportunity that they'd only ever wanted two children and had both agreed they wouldn't have any more, and seemed incapable of understanding what the problem was. There were times when she wondered if she was being unreasonable, and if perhaps he was right. But she soon came to realise that feelings can't be wrong. It was the lack of control over her own body and her own choices that hurt the most, and there would be no coming back from that. It was something she might get used to, and which would probably ease with time, but it would never be reversible or solvable.

The hormone tablets were supposed to make things easier, but all they'd done was make her feel more unbalanced. She knew it would take time to get used to her new body, and for balance to be achieved. But there were days — like today – when it felt like that was a long way off.

'Right, grub's up,' Mark said, poking his head through the doorway into the living room. 'You want a hand?'

Caroline sighed. 'It's fine. I'm not an invalid.' She looked at him, immediately regretting her words. 'I'm sorry. It's been a long day, that's all. Sorry. I know you're only trying to help. But really, I can stand up on my own.'

She followed Mark through into the dining room and sat down. Although she'd felt hungry only moments earlier, now the sight of food make her feel sick. She smiled at Mark and forced a mouthful, chewing it over and over as she tried to summon up the courage to swallow the food.

'You okay?' he asked a minute or two later.

Caroline nodded. 'Mmmhmm.'

'Did I overcook it?'

'No. It's good.'

'Only you've been chewing it for ages.'

Caroline swallowed. 'It's fine. Honestly.' She looked back down at her plate. Another mouthful seemed far more daunting than it had any right to. There was no way she could eat even a fraction of what was on her plate.

'You don't have to eat it, you know. I won't be offended.'

'The food's fine, Mark. There's nothing wrong with the food.'

Mark nodded. 'Okay. Not hungry?'

'No, I am. I was. I just…'

'Don't worry about it.'

'Well I am worried about it, because now you're upset with me.'

'I'm not.'

'You are. You only say you're not when you are.'

'What the hell? That makes no sense at all.'

She looked back at the plate of food. 'And now you're angry.'

'I'm confused, Caz. I don't have a clue what's going on. Have I done something?'

She tensed her jaw. 'No, Mark. Not everything stems from you.'

Mark threw his fork down on the plate. 'Well there's no need for that. I'm only trying to help you. Support you. But whatever I do, I seem to get it in the neck.'

She got the impression that nothing she could say now would make things better. The situation had got too tense, too confused, and even trying to smooth things over would only cause more aggravation.

'It's probably just the tablets,' she said. 'It's been a long day. I think I'm just going to go to bed.'

Without waiting for a response, Caroline pushed her chair back, stood up and headed for the stairs.

14

Caroline arrived at the hospital the next morning feeling apprehensive. If she was honest with herself and managed to cut through the internal panic, she felt as though she'd beaten the cancer. In many ways, she felt better than she had in a long time, but she still couldn't shake that horrible nagging doubt at the back of her mind. She'd felt relatively fine in the early stages of the disease. What was to say this wasn't the same situation all over again?

Her post-surgery scan had been delayed a little due to a combination of Christmas and chronic underfunding of local health services, but she hadn't minded too much. In a way, not knowing had provided her with relief. But there was a growing sense that she needed to know. The clarity that would come from a definitive answer would allow her to move on.

After she was called through, she was asked a few questions about how she'd been after her surgery. They seemed surprised that she'd been back at work — as did most people — and although she was tempted to tell them to mind their own business, she instead politely pointed out that she felt just fine, and that she hadn't been taking on anything too taxing. If pushed, she'd happily explain how sitting around at home doing nothing would be a whole lot riskier.

'How are the energy levels doing?' the nurse asked.

'Fine. I mean, I'm not sure I remember what "normal" is, but I certainly feel a hell of a lot better than I have in the last year or so.'

'Good. Well, the notes seem to indicate the surgery went well from a practical point of view, but what we're going to do today is an MRI scan. It's very similar to the CT scan you had pre-diagnosis, insofar as we lay you down and slide you into a weird white tube, but the MRI will give us a more detailed image of what's going on. It just means that if there are any signs of regrowth — even small ones — we should be able to see them and do something about them. Does that all make sense?'

Caroline let out a small laugh. 'To be honest, you can do whatever you like as long as you get rid of it.'

The nurse gave a friendly smile laced with the slightest touch of *I've-heard-that-one-a-thousand-times-before-but-I'll-humour-you-anyway*. 'With a little bit of luck, it should all be gone already, but we'll soon know.'

'How soon?' Caroline asked. 'I don't know if anyone actually mentioned that to me. Sorry if they did.'

'It depends. You'll get a letter within the next few days

with a date for a follow-up appointment. By that time we should have the results and we'll be able to talk about the next steps, continued monitoring, all that sort of thing. Shall we get cracking?'

Caroline looked through the window towards the MRI scanner. It was an odd feeling, knowing that machine would — quite literally — dictate her future. It would either signal the success of the surgery and a new start, or something else entirely. With her heart beating heavily and a soaring sense of trepidation, she stood and followed the nurse.

15

Less than an hour later, Caroline was back in work mode, having buried her health worries in the back of her mind. She was in Uppingham, at the premises of Allure Design, having picked Dexter up on the way. She'd been surprised to find Monique — despite her release from custody — nowhere to be seen.

Caroline didn't like to stereotype, but she was fairly certain she could've picked Tom Mackintosh out of a line-up of potential IT managers. His grey t-shirt was at least two sizes too big for his lanky frame, and the frayed bottoms of his jeans declared they'd seen better days. As she got closer, she noticed he smelled of stale smoke, although somewhat sweeter. She wondered if it wasn't purely tobacco he'd been smoking, or if her sense of smell was still recovering from heavy chemotherapy. Right now, though, she had more important matters on her mind.

'Good to meet you, Tom,' Caroline said, shaking his hand. 'How was the break?'

'Lovely, thanks. Always good to get away.'

'Anywhere nice?'

'Up to Scotland. Love it there.'

Caroline winced. 'Crikey, it must've been cold up there. It's bad enough down here.'

'Exactly,' Tom replied, with a know-all smile. 'I'm a big fan of all-weather camping. I love all the survivalist stuff. No better way to get away from it all than be in the middle of nowhere for a bit. The cold just gives it an extra edge.'

She couldn't deny that sounded like heaven at times. 'Not that we're ever far from the middle of nowhere round here,' she said.

'Oh, definitely. In fact, if it's something you're keen on, there are some great local places I go to. Fineshade and Wakerley Woods are brilliant. Whack a tent in a bag, kit up and off you go. They've both got facilities if you want them, and if you know the right spots you can even get wi-fi.'

'I couldn't think of anything worse. Especially in this weather.'

'Ah, you're missing out. Get yourself down to Fineshade and hire a Danish shelter. Basically a tiny three-sided log cabin with a fire pit outside. Beautiful.'

'I'll think about it,' Caroline said, tickled by his enthusiasm. 'Still, sorry to burst your bubble.'

'Indeed. This isn't really what I expected to come back to, I'll be honest, but I'll do what I can to help.'

Caroline smiled. 'Looks like they're a bit stuck without you. What happens if something goes down while you're away?'

'To be honest, there isn't really anything much that *can* go down. If there are network problems it's usually down to our internet service provider, if the website collapses it's down to the designer or the host, and if someone forgets their computer password for the sixth time that month — well, that's their problem, isn't it?' Tom replied, smiling.

'Sounds familiar,' Dexter said, looking at Caroline.

'So, how can I help?' Tom asked.

Caroline took a deep breath and considered her wording carefully. 'Well, at the moment it's more a case of gathering evidence. We don't have our eyes on anything specific, but there's always the slightest possibility there might be some digital evidence somewhere. We've got a specialist en route who'll explain things and let you know what we need. Essentially, it'll involve making copies of systems and communications. It's all beyond me, so I'll leave him to explain. He should be here any minute.'

Tom shrugged. 'Alright. Do you guys want a drink or something in the meantime? Tea? Coffee?'

Caroline smiled. 'Coffee would be lovely, thanks.'

'Sounds good,' Dexter replied.

They followed Tom through the office towards the brightly decorated break room, where Caroline eyed up the egg chairs once again. 'Y'know,' she said, 'these things do start to grow on you, don't they?'

'Not really my style,' Tom replied, leaving Caroline

wondering what his style actually was. The closest she could come to defining it was "greasy".

'So, what kind of guy was Martin? Good boss?' Dexter asked.

'Yeah, he's alright. Was. Crikey, feels weird saying that.'

'I imagine it'll take some getting used to. What were his relationships like, do you know?'

'Relationships?'

'Yeah. Did he get on with everyone?'

'Oh. Right. Yeah, sorry, I thought you meant... Sorry.'

'Meant what, Tom?'

'I don't want to drop anyone in it. It's just... there were rumours. About him and Monique,' he said, almost silently mouthing her name although she was nowhere to be seen.

'What about them?' Caroline asked innocently.

'Probably just rumours. But office gossip was that they were, well, you know.'

'I think I do, yes.'

'I dunno what'll happen to our jobs now. Someone said his wife's a director too, but I don't think I'd recognise her if she walked in here. Can't see she'll be too bothered about keeping the place going.'

'You never know. She might bring in a manager or bump someone up to looking after the place. Silent director sort of thing.'

Tom laughed. 'Chance'll be a fine thing. Never much silence round here, I can tell you that.'

'One of your colleagues mentioned that Martin had a bit of a row with someone last week,' Caroline said. 'Did you hear anything?'

'Ah. Yeah, I think I know the one you mean. It was the day before I went up to Scotland. Thursday, it would've been. I didn't really hear what was said, but it didn't sound good.'

'Do you know what it was about?'

Tom shook his head. 'No, sorry. To be honest, stuff like that happens at work sometimes. There won't be anything in it.'

'Who was he arguing with?'

'Uh, Amie, I think.'

'How well do you know Amie? What's she like?'

Tom took a deep breath, then let out a huge sigh. 'I dunno. I mean, she's fine. She's nice. She seems to get on well with everyone. Keeps herself to herself, mostly. She can be difficult to get to know, but not necessarily in a bad way, if you know what I mean. Private. But cheerful, friendly, bubbly.'

'This is Amie Tanner?' Caroline asked, unable to reconcile Tom's description with the woman they'd already met.

'Yeah. Why?'

'Just trying to build a picture,' Caroline replied, smiling. 'How were things left after the argument?'

'How do you mean?'

'Well, did Amie stick around or did she go home?

Were there any comments or remarks made? Did they kiss and make up?'

'Nothing specific that I can remember. They seemed fine, I think. No permanent falling out, if that's what you mean. I don't imagine Martin would stay angry at her for long.'

Caroline cocked her head slightly as she registered this comment. 'How do you mean?'

Tom looked as though he'd just realised he'd said too much. 'Oh, nothing,' he said.

'No, go on.'

'Honestly, it's nothing. It's probably not even relevant.'

Dexter interjected. 'With the greatest of respect, that's for us to decide.'

Tom looked at him, then back at Caroline. 'It's just... Well, it's difficult to explain really. It's Martin. Between you and me, I think he'd been trying it on with Amie as well. It's the sort of guy he is. Was.'

'A relationship, you mean?'

'Oh no. Not Amie. I doubt it, anyway. She's always been pretty smitten with her other half. Not that he's the nicest guy in the world, from what I've seen. But Martin had a bit of a reputation. It was a sort of unspoken thing. Especially with... you know.'

'His wife?'

'Well, yeah. No-one really wanted to rock the boat, I guess. But like I say, they got along fine. Everyone has arguments every now and again, but it all seemed to be sorted out pretty quickly. And I doubt it had anything to do with what happened.'

Caroline smiled at him. She had to admire his optimism, but she wasn't entirely sure she agreed.

16

Meanwhile, Sara and Aidan had taken a drive over to Seaton to speak with Sandra Forbes. They'd been at the George & Dragon the previous day and had seen how uncomfortable the owner had looked when they'd asked about Martin, and they were keen to try and gauge how much Sandra really knew about her husband's extra-curricular activities.

'She must have known,' Aidan said, thinking to himself as Sara drove. 'If it was going on for that long, there's no way she was oblivious to it all. Especially if they were right at the pub about her reaction when she came looking for him.'

'We'll soon see. It's the timing that worries me,' Sara replied. 'Just enough time from discovering the truth to have sat and stewed on it for a bit before planning her way out.'

'You think she did him in because he was having an affair?'

'Honestly? I've no idea. But we probably shouldn't go into this with too many preconceptions or theories. If we do that, we'll only see what we want to see.'

'Fair point,' Aidan replied, returning to his own thoughts.

A few minutes later, they arrived at Sandra Forbes's house in Seaton, and were soon seated in her living room.

'We're really sorry to intrude on you again at such a difficult time,' Sara said, 'but we're at the stage now where we're looking to widen the investigation. That means we need to find out more about Martin's friends and contacts, his work, all that sort of thing.'

Sandra gave a non-committal shrug. She looked as though she'd barely slept, which was hardly surprising. 'I'll help if I can, but he tended to keep most things to himself.'

Was there a hint of something in those words? Sara thought perhaps there had been, but she silently reminded herself not to look for things that might not be there.

'Okay, well let's start with work. I understand you're a director of Allure. Were you involved in the company much before Martin died?'

Sandra shook her head. 'No, not really. I mean, I was listed as a director, but that was only to split the income and halve the tax bill. Totally legal and above board.'

'Don't worry, I'm not the tax inspector,' Sara said,

smiling. 'Did Martin talk much about the people he worked with?'

'Not really. Sometimes, perhaps. But he was pretty good at keeping his work and home life separate. As far as he was concerned, he closed the door and went home at the end of the day and that was that. He spent a huge amount of time working, but didn't talk about it when he was at home.'

'Very sensible,' Sara replied. 'I wish I could compartmentalise like that. What about colleagues? Did he ever see them socially outside work?'

'Oh no, never. I mean, there were work Christmas events and things like that, but he never made friends with anyone that worked for him. That can be a very slippery slope.'

Sandra's response was a little too forceful for Sara's liking. In any case, she wasn't so sure she agreed.

'Makes sense. Did you ever meet any of his colleagues and employees?'

Sandra shook her head. 'Not really. One or two.'

'How about Amie Tanner?'

Sandra shrugged. 'I think I know the one you mean, but I'm not sure if we've met.'

'There's a woman there called Monique, do you know her?'

There was a flash of something in Sandra's eyes. 'No. Not really. Name rings a vague bell.'

'She's the one who thinks she's Cicero.'

'Like I say, I never really paid much attention. Why are you only asking about the women?'

'I'm just trying to get some background. Look, I'm afraid I'm going to have to ask some difficult questions. I know they might be uncomfortable, and the answer might very well be "no". That's fine. We just need to cover all angles and make sure we've got all the information we need.'

Sandra sighed and spoke quietly. 'If you're going to ask me whether Martin had a relationship with any of his female staff, I can tell you now I don't know. I don't think so. You'd think a woman would know if something was going on, wouldn't you? But no. I think I can at least do him the good grace of assuming he was always the kind, honourable and good man I knew.'

Sara nodded slowly. 'Okay. That's all fine and completely understandable. We just want to help get justice for Martin. And for you. I want to ask about Martin's leisure time, if I can please. I gather he was a keen runner. Did he have any other hobbies at all?'

'No. He didn't really have time for much else. He worked all day, went for a run in the evenings then either crashed out in front of the telly or stayed out for a couple of drinks.'

'Ah yes. At the George & Dragon, isn't it? The one at the other end of the village.'

'Yes.'

'Nice place. Aidan and I popped in yesterday lunchtime, actually. Do you know the owners well?'

Sandra shrugged again. 'Not really. We've been in a few times for meals and things, but Martin tended to prefer to keep himself to himself.'

Or to Monique Dupont, Sara thought.

'I presume he must've been pretty familiar to them, though? If he often went in after his runs, I mean. You'd imagine they'd recognise him as a local.'

'I don't know. I'd like to think so. Look, I don't mean to sound rude but do you know how much longer this is likely to take? I'm really not sure I can be of much use to you, and my sister and her husband are due to arrive from Cornwall shortly.'

'That's okay. We won't keep you too much longer,' Sara said, smiling. 'The reason I mention it is because we asked in the pub about Martin. Just trying to build up a picture of him as a person. They didn't seem to really know him at all.'

Sandra swallowed. 'Like I say, Martin liked to keep himself to himself. I doubt he was on first-name terms with the staff.'

'No, but they're always aware of who they've got in. They said they thought he'd been in once or twice before, but he wasn't a regular by any means. They couldn't even pinpoint when he'd last been in, but they reckoned it'd been weeks.'

Sandra started to blink rapidly. 'Maybe the staff were new. Or perhaps you showed them an old photo. I don't know.'

'It was this photo,' Sara said, showing it to her. 'A fairly recent one of the two of you. Christmas or New Year, it looks like.'

'New Year's Eve.'

'Pretty good likeness of Martin?'

Sandra flicked her eyes towards the photo, then off towards the fireplace. 'Not bad.'

'The staff at the pub were certain we were talking about the same person. They knew who he was, but were adamant they hadn't seen him in a while. They recognised you, though.'

There was a visible reaction from Sandra. There'd been a smaller one when she'd looked at the photo and must have known this was coming, but now it was clear to both Sara and Aidan.

'When did you last visit the George & Dragon, Sandra?' Sara asked.

'I… I don't remember. Like I said, I don't exactly go there often.'

'No, they mentioned that. They said you weren't a regular either, but they distinctly recalled that you'd been in recently. Does that ring any bells?'

Sandra looked up towards the ceiling, seemingly having accepted they already knew the truth. Finally, she lowered her head, sighed and spoke.

'I went in there a couple of weeks back. I'd expected him home and he didn't arrive, so I went down there because that's where I thought he'd be.'

'But he wasn't.'

'No.'

'Do you know where he was?'

Sandra swallowed. 'No.'

'Did you ask him?'

'No.'

'Why not?'

'Because I didn't want to know, alright?' Sandra replied, her voice louder and more forceful. 'Of course I knew he wasn't going to the bloody pub all the time. I'm not stupid. I knew there was something else going on. I didn't want details. I didn't want names. I just wanted to know I wasn't going absolutely bloody mad.'

'I can understand that,' Sara said, trying to calm the situation. 'Did you have any theories? Suspicions as to where he might have been?'

'With a woman, obviously. You don't need me to spell that out for you.'

'Which woman?'

'I don't know. I really don't know.'

'Okay. A friend? Someone he'd met in the pub? Someone from work?'

'I don't know. I said I don't know. I don't want to know, either. Even good people don't always make the right decisions. It doesn't make them bad people. Martin was a good person. And if you don't mind, that's the way I'd like to remember him.'

17

Not long after Tom's revelation about Martin and Amie, the digital forensics specialist arrived at Allure's offices to back up and copy their computer systems. Knowing it was likely to take some time, and with bigger fish to fry, Caroline and Dexter made the decision to head over to Amie Tanner's house for a surprise visit.

They hadn't planned to spend the day ping-ponging across Rutland, but they found themselves once again on the Uppingham to Oakham road, bypassing the county town before veering off towards Market Overton, where Amie Tanner lived with her family.

'It was a bit weird, that,' Dexter said, not long after they'd set off. 'I mean, the way he described Amie, saying how bubbly and friendly she was.'

'Maybe we caught her on a bad day yesterday. Maybe she doesn't like the police. Maybe it's her way of dealing with grief. Maybe that's Tom's idea of bubbly. Who knows?'

'True. But I know you clocked it too. I could see the look on your face.'

Caroline let out a small chuckle. 'One thing you learn quite quickly in this job, Dex, is there's no such thing as normal. Just because you or I might describe someone in a certain way, or because we'd have our own methods of doing things, it doesn't mean everyone else would agree.'

Dexter looked at her. 'Is that you trying to be philosophical?'

'Maybe. Why?'

'Because it was terrible.'

Caroline laughed again. 'Alright, I'll keep it to myself next time. You're right on one thing, though. Something doesn't quite seem to be adding up, does it?'

Dexter put his hand on his chest in mock offence. 'What? Secrets, rumours and hidden scandals? In Rutland? Well I never.'

'I know. Who would've guessed?'

'So what's your theory?' Dexter asked. 'Amie and Martin have been shagging, they've had a falling out, he's threatened to tell her husband and she's finished him off?'

'Nice choice of words. But I doubt it's that straightforward. Why would Martin want to reveal all? He had as much to lose as she did. More, if you count his affair with Monique and god knows who else on top.'

'What's that you were saying about nice choice of words?'

Caroline smiled. 'You know what I meant. Rare to get a woman killing a man, too, and almost never violently.'

'I'd like to see a non-violent murder.'

'Yes, but I mean women tend to poison or set up accidents.'

'Sounds pretty violent to me. What if Amie was being coerced or forced into stuff like Monique was? Maybe Amie's husband found out? Got jealous, killed Martin, Amie worked out what'd happened and decided to cover for her husband to hide what'd happened.'

Caroline chuckled. 'I think we should probably meet him and speak to him first, before accusing him of murder, don't you?'

Dexter made a murmuring noise in return. 'Alright, spoilsport.'

18

They arrived at Amie Tanner's house in Market Overton about twenty minutes later, the low sun bright in the sky as the frosty start to the day had begun to thaw.

They parked up in a bay opposite the Black Bull pub, the Church of St Peter and St Paul just visible through the bare branches of the trees between. The car fell silent as Caroline switched off the engine and the sound of the hot-air blowers suddenly stopped.

'Walk from here?' she said. 'Good to get some air in the lungs. Plus we can sneak up like Cagney and Lacey.'

'Which one am I?' Dexter asked.

'I'll leave that to your filthy imagination.'

The pair walked down Thistleton Road towards Amie Tanner's house, their hands thrust in their coat pockets as the biting cold threatened to worm its way in.

'Christ, it's even colder here than it was in Uppingham,' Dexter said. 'How's that even possible?'

'Because that was Uppingham. We're up north now,' Caroline replied with a grin.

A couple of minutes later, they reached Amie Tanner's house and Dexter knocked on the door. They could see the edge of the TV screen through the living room window — a kids' programme Caroline didn't recognise. A few moments later, the door opened.

'Amie, hi,' Caroline said. 'DI Caroline Hills and DS Dexter Antoine. We spoke yesterday.'

'I know. Hardly going to forget that, am I? Can I help you?'

'We just wondered if we might be able to pop in and have a quick word.'

'Have you found out who did it?'

'Not yet. We need some more information.'

Amie let out a sigh. 'Alright. But I warn you, the place is a mess.'

They stepped inside and closed the door behind them. Dexter glanced into the living room, briefly locking eyes with Amie's husband. 'Morning,' he said. 'Sorry to trouble you.'

'It's fine,' he replied. 'I'll keep the girls in here. They're glued to the telly anyway.'

Amie led them through into the kitchen and gestured towards the table for them to sit. 'Tea? Coffee?'

Caroline raised a hand. 'We're fine, thanks. We'll try not to take up too much of your time. We can see you're busy. We just wanted to ask you a couple more questions about Martin Forbes. Somewhere private, perhaps?'

Amie looked at them for a moment, then poked her head round the door into the living room. 'Gavin? Can you take the girls upstairs for a bit please?'

They listened as Amie's husband did as he was asked, before Caroline spoke quietly enough to ensure they wouldn't be overheard.

'I'll get straight to the point. We've had some reports that your relationship with Martin wasn't always strictly work-related. Is that true?'

Amie laughed. 'Is that what you wanted to ask me? Jesus Christ, of course not. No chance.'

'There was never anything other than a working relationship?' Caroline asked.

'Absolutely not, no. If someone's tried telling you that, they've got the wrong end of the stick completely. He tried coming on to me a few times, but I always brushed him off. I'm married with kids, for Christ's sake.'

'And it never went any further than Martin's advances and your rejections?'

'No. Categorically no.'

Caroline nodded as she wrote in her notebook. 'Okay. Sorry. You understand we have to ask these things, of course.' Amie didn't reply. 'Ooh, I like those,' Caroline said, nodding her head towards the vase on the kitchen windowsill. 'Are they roses? They're very dark.'

Amie's demeanour seemed to change almost immediately. 'Yes. Rosa Black Baccara.'

'You seem to have quite a lot of admirers.'

'Actually, they were my dad's favourite. He used to be a

gardener at Barnsdale. Every year he used to send me a dozen of them on Valentine's Day.'

'Used to?'

'He died. Ten years ago. I think my mum sends them now, but she'll never admit it. I thought it was Gavin at first, but it's not. I can always tell when he's lying. I suppose I might never find out, but that doesn't matter. It's sort of a reminder of Dad. It's nice.'

'It is. Sorry, I didn't mean to—'

'It's fine.'

'They're an interesting colour. I've never seen roses that dark before.'

Amie shrugged. 'I guess that's why he liked them. He loved anything that was different, out of the ordinary. He was a bit of an old hippy, in many ways.'

'Man after my own heart. So, let's go back to Monday night. You weren't at work, is that right?'

'Yes. I've got the week off.'

'Were you at home?'

'Yes. We went into Peterborough on Saturday, but we've been at home since. Gavin's been out to walk the dog a couple of times, but that's about it.'

'In the village?'

'Yes.'

Caroline nodded and noted this down. Market Overton was a good half an hour's drive from where Martin's body was found. 'And what time did he go out on Monday?'

Amie laughed. 'About lunchtime. Sorry, but you're on

the wrong track if you think Gavin had anything to do with it.'

'We're just trying to ascertain everyone's whereabouts, that's all.'

'Okay, well in that case we were both here, at home. All evening.'

'What were you doing?'

Amie sighed. 'We put the kids to bed, then I had a bath for an hour or so, then I came downstairs, we opened a bottle of wine and we had sex on the sofa. Is that enough information for you?'

'Where was he while you were in the bath?'

'Downstairs, watching TV. And before you ask, yes, I know he was because he's allergic to the dog and he was sneezing almost constantly. Besides which, the car's parked right below our bathroom window so I would've heard him if he'd gone out, and it's a bloody long walk to Seaton.'

'Okay, I think we all need to take a breather for a few moments,' Caroline said, trying to sound as soothing as possible. 'I understand it's a difficult time and we might not be coming across in the right way, but I just want to assure you that all we're trying to do is get all the information we can as quickly and efficiently as possible so we can find Martin's killer.'

Amie nodded and looked up at her. 'Well in that case, you'd better get back out there, because you're not going to find them here.'

19

'We can verify everything with cell site info,' Dexter said as they walked back to Caroline's car. 'We'll be able to see if either of them left the house. The car's brand new, too. That'll have a tracker on it.'

'We won't get authorisation to access that. We're nowhere near the evidence threshold.'

'Seriously?'

'Afraid so. Vehicles are classed as premises, so it'd count as property interference. We'd need part 3 RIPA authority. Chief Constable territory, that. We won't get it.'

'If the car's classed as premises, can't we just get a search warrant under PACE?'

'Only if you fancy convincing a magistrate that we've got solid grounds for suspecting Amie.'

Dexter raised an eyebrow. 'Does that mean you think she didn't do it?'

Caroline sighed. 'Honestly? I don't know. I don't think

she was lying. But that doesn't change the fact that something doesn't quite seem right.'

'Yeah, but if Martin Forbes definitely died on Monday night and Amie and Gavin Tanner definitely didn't leave their house on Monday night, what else can we do? If the evidence says it can't be them, it can't be them.'

'It doesn't mean they're not involved. Monique Dupont was a solid suspect too, until an alibi popped up. What if that *is* the connection? What if they're working together? We need to dig deeper. Find out more about them, their connections. They could've paid someone else to do it.'

'I don't think that's likely, do you?' Dexter asked. 'There are plenty of angles here. Martin Forbes seems to have pissed enough people off along the line. We had Monique Dupont pretty much nailed on at one point, don't forget.'

'None of this is likely, Dex. Nothing. It's not likely you'll go out for a jog and get beaten to death under a viaduct, but try telling that to Martin Forbes.'

'Even so, I don't think I'm fully on board with the Tanners being gangland kingpins who can just drop twenty grand and phone in a hit. They're not the Market Overton Mafia.'

Caroline picked up the pace, wanting to get back to the relative warmth of her car, desperate to return to the office and fill up on black coffee. The peaks and troughs of energy and fatigue were proving difficult to get used to, but there was no way she was going to let on to anyone that she was anything other than absolutely fine.

It'd taken a while for her to work her way around it, but she'd grown adept at managing her symptoms and masking the severity of her exhaustion from just about everyone around her. She knew it probably wasn't healthy, but then again neither was lying around in bed all day. The sheer boredom had left her on the verge of going mad, and she was in no doubt it'd be far healthier in the long run to get back on her feet.

'As much as I'd love the Market Overton Mafia to exist,' she said, 'I'm inclined to agree it's probably not going to be our primary line of inquiry. Would certainly make the job one hell of a lot more interesting, though. I can just see you sliding over car bonnets and gunning down speedboats full of drug-runners on Rutland Water.'

'Never say never,' Dexter replied, beaming.

'You agree there's definitely something up with the Tanners, though?'

Dexter shrugged. 'I dunno. Maybe they're just a bit weird. You get people like that, where something seems off but they haven't actually done anything wrong. That's half the fun of the job.'

'Fun? Frustration, more like.'

'Yeah, but we can't just go around nicking people because they seem like wrong'uns. That's why we deal with evidence and facts rather than old-school coppers' instincts.'

Caroline grunted. 'Yeah, alright. I don't need the

lecture. I'm not suggesting we ignore evidence and facts. I just... There's definitely something not right there. And I don't want to lose track of that, then find out later we've missed something really obvious.'

Dexter smiled as they reached the car. 'Okay. I promise you I won't forget you think Amie Tanner's a wrong'un. How about that?'

Caroline returned a wry smile. 'Hmmm. Deal.'

20

The black coffee almost scalded her throat, but she didn't care. Warmth was warmth, and right now she would take anything she could get.

She'd lost quite a bit of weight over the past weeks and months — more than she could account for through simply lying in bed for much of it — and it'd shocked her to see how much the treatment had taken out of her. It was cold — abnormally cold — but Caroline was in no doubt that she was feeling it more than she would have done in any other year.

She'd joked with her colleagues about London being perpetually five degrees warmer than the rest of the country, but it'd only been a partial joke. Snow and frost had been rarities, and where they occurred they tended to be gone before breakfast. The cold had been damp, dreary and miserable. Here, it seemed to bite. It was a bitter, inescapable cold. A thin, sharp chill that managed to creep its way into every crevice of your clothing. Unrelenting.

She supposed it was the openness of the area. London was built up, buildings crammed together, central heating seeping out of walls every few feet; sunlight bouncing off glass towers and warming up the streets; cars and trucks sitting in traffic jams, their warm exhaust fumes defrosting the tarmac. There was none of that here. This was pure.

The cold was one thing. She could deal with that. But, try as she might, the one thing she couldn't quite get used to was the quiet. Even in the middle of Oakham or Uppingham — as busy as the county got — it was nothing compared to what she was used to. Things were still. Calm. And now she was more convinced than ever that everything was somehow interlinked. Causational, even. It was as if the calm, still air had frozen far harsher than the boisterous, moving air of London ever could.

It was almost ironic, the family moving to Rutland to escape the noise and enjoy the great outdoors, only to spend weeks and months on end in the house — or, in Caroline's case, in bed — the second the weather turned.

She told herself she'd suggest to Mark that they start walking or cycling again, provided she could summon up the energy. There was a certain attraction in bare trees and frost-glazed fields that couldn't be matched by even the most sumptuous of summers. Besides which, she needed the exercise. She was sure a large part of her lethargy and fatigue was due to having done very little for weeks on end. For now, though, there were more pressing matters to attend to.

'Okay,' she said, as she perched on the edge of a desk. 'Welcome to today's afternoon briefing on Operation Cruickshank.' It always felt a little daft in her mind to speak so formally to just three other officers, but years of Met training and habits were hard to shake off. 'First things first. You'll be aware by now that the suspect we had in custody, Monique Dupont, has been released without charge. She's got a solid alibi for the night of the murder, which has been backed up with CCTV evidence.

'Dexter and I have been out and about this morning speaking to people who knew Martin Forbes. We went back to the offices of Allure Design to speak to their IT manager, Tom Mackintosh, primarily to obtain potential digital evidence, but also to speak to him as a work colleague of Martin's. The most interesting part was the revelation that Martin Forbes had been trying it on with Amie Tanner. Tom said it was something that was never actually spoken about, but which a few people had cottoned on to. We spoke to Amie Tanner again, and she said Martin had tried coming on to her a few times, but that she'd always rejected him. Then again, she was saying that while she was sitting in her kitchen with her husband and kids upstairs. Between the four of us, I got the distinct impression there was more to it than Amie Tanner was making out. Whenever Dex and I've spoken to her she's been cold, clipped, almost rude. Everyone else seems to think she's friendly and bubbly. There's something not quite right there, and I don't think it's just a dislike of the police. For now, she remains a definite person of interest.'

'A suspect?' Aidan asked.

Caroline took a deep breath before speaking. 'At this stage, I'm not willing to rule her out. She has an alibi in her husband, but we don't know they're not in on it together. I don't imagine for one minute they both went out and killed Martin Forbes, because they had the kids asleep in the house. Aidan, can you check cell site data for their mobile phones? Let's see if we can at least prove where their phones were. Let's arrange for the neighbours to get a knock on the door, too. Covertly, if you can. See if any of them saw one of the Tanners coming or going from the house on the night Martin Forbes died. Dex?'

'Nothing much to add, other than — for what it's worth — I don't think Amie or Gavin Tanner did it. My reading of the situation was similar, but I wonder if perhaps Amie disliked Martin Forbes so much she's actually quite pleased he's gone. That'd explain why she was keen to prove she wasn't involved, but not too bothered about helping identify his killer.'

'No, but even so, keeping information from us is an offence in itself,' Caroline said. 'So we need to make sure what she says is absolutely watertight. If she's keeping something from us that could prejudice the investigation, we'll come down on her like a ton of bricks. I know she's hiding something. We just need to get to the bottom of what that is.'

21

Caroline headed home early that afternoon, having told her team she had another appointment. It wasn't strictly true: the only appointment she had was with her sofa and a glass of wine. Even so, she could legitimately argue it was a medical appointment, and there was no doubt whatsoever in her mind that she absolutely needed the extra rest if she was going to be able to see out this investigation.

One of the things she'd noticed creeping in recently was a distinct lack of patience and a growing irritability with almost everything. It wasn't her usual style, but it wasn't entirely new, either. She'd first noticed it a few months earlier, and it had continued to grow since. She supposed it was a result of a few things: uprooting the family and moving to Rutland, living with cancer, dealing with the fallout of her recovery. There'd been more than enough stressors to give her concern for her own mental state, and sometimes she felt as if she was unable to cope with it.

The boys had been great that afternoon. They seemed to know when she was at her worst and gave her the space she needed. Mark, on the other hand, had continued to misjudge.

He meant well — she knew that — but it was infuriating how often she needed to tell him she was fine, no she didn't want another cup of tea, no she didn't need a hot water bottle and yes, the volume on the TV was absolutely fine, just as it was thirty seconds earlier. She knew he was only trying to help, but she found his constant check-ups and questions were draining far more energy from her than anything else, and she wondered if it might have been more conducive to her recovery to have simply stayed at work.

Still, with the boys now tucked up in bed, she'd be able to head up herself before long and get some sleep. Mark was watching a documentary about the Second World War, mistakenly thinking she was interested. In reality, she didn't have the energy to think of anything else to watch and was content enough just staring at the screen.

'I might head up,' she said as the documentary cut to yet another commercial break. There were only so many adverts for stairlifts and commemorative gold coins she could handle in one evening.

'Oh,' Mark replied, a simple sound that conveyed more disappointment than an entire Jeffrey Archer novel.

'What?'

'Nothing. I just thought it might be nice to spend some time together, that's all.'

'We have been spending time together. I came home early.'

'Yeah, but I've barely seen you, have I? You've been in here, I've been sorting the boys out.'

Caroline couldn't help but laugh, although she feared it might have sounded a little condescending. 'Come off it, Mark. You've barely left me alone for ten seconds without badgering me.'

'Badgering you? What, by checking you're alright and seeing if you needed anything?'

'I'm not being funny, but I've spent the day at work, running a murder investigation team. I can handle getting myself a cup of tea.'

'Alright, fine. Suit yourself.'

'What now?'

Mark was resolute in his refusal to answer. 'Nothing,' he said.

'No, come on. What have I done?'

'It's more what you haven't done,' Mark replied. 'You've got people around you who care for you and want to help you, and all you do is throw it back in our faces. Jesus, I've never known anyone get so angry about not having to do any household chores, and who's told all they have to do is sit and watch TV. But no, even that needs an argument.'

Caroline sighed. 'I didn't start an argument, Mark. All I said was I was going to go up to bed. I'm tired. I'm recovering from surgery. I've not been back at work long and it's taking it out of me. If you want to show concern, forget the tea and biscuits and just give me the mental space I need to get back on my feet, alright?'

'Fine. Whatever,' Mark said, standing up and leaving the room.

'Oh, come on,' Caroline called, before the ringing of her phone disturbed her. She looked at the screen. It was Sara Henshaw.

22

It never ceased to amaze Caroline how interlinked mental and physical energy were. Even though she'd felt ready to sleep for weeks, the call from Sara Henshaw had provided a boost of energy like no other.

Her car hit the speed bumps along Ashwell Road a little harder than usual as she headed back to work, keen to see for herself what Sara had uncovered.

Sara could go on to big things — if she wanted to. Caroline was sure of that. But there was a clear lack of confidence in her, a sense that she didn't appreciate her talents and value to the team anywhere near as much as others did. That was often the case in policing. The culture, stress and sheer lack of time meant positive reinforcement often fell by the wayside. Despite this, Sara always seemed to come up with the goods.

Caroline parked her car in the small car park at the front of the police station and headed inside.

'You should have been home hours ago,' she said when she found Sara in the office.

Sara simply shrugged. 'Plenty to be doing. Anyway. Not much point going back to an empty flat, is there?'

Caroline thought she detected a hint of sadness in her eyes. She wasn't one to pry into her colleagues' private lives, but she'd got the distinct impression Sara had been single for some time, and that it wasn't a situation she was entirely happy with. She made a mental note to have a chat with her when the time was right. 'Well, I appreciate the dedication,' she replied. 'What have you found?'

Sara sat down at her desk as Caroline stood behind her. 'Well,' she said, 'I've been doing some digging into Amie Tanner, like you asked. It seems she's got a pretty colourful past.'

'I see. Go on.'

'It's looking like she's a bit of a bad luck charm, to say the least. We already know she lost her dad ten years ago. But five years before that, Amie — Amie Murray as she was then — was seeing a bloke called Russell Speakman. Until he died.'

'Died? What were the circumstances?'

'Suspicious. He fell down the stairs at home. The cause of death was given as cranio-cerebral trauma and intra-thoracic visceral injuries.'

'In English?'

'From what I can make out, he cracked his skull open and broke a rib, which pierced his lung.'

'Christ. I'll be walking down the stairs more carefully in future.'

'It's a weird one. The stairs were uncarpeted and there were hard floors upstairs and down, which won't have helped. Pretty steep stairs, too, according to the report. But it also shows that he tumbled as he fell and hit his head at least twice. I don't know about you, but I've slipped down the stairs a few times before and I always end up a few steps further down on my arse. I don't go bouncing around like a tumble dryer ball. Even if he fell awkwardly, how likely is it that a grown adult male will manage to do that much damage to himself?'

'Was he under the influence of anything?' Caroline asked.

Sara shook her head. 'Toxicology all clear.'

'And what are the odds of him falling like that? Do you know?'

Sara shrugged. 'No idea, but I wouldn't put money on them. The report says as much itself, but the coroner's verdict was accidental death. There were no other suspicious circumstances.'

'And what about Amie? Where was she?'

'Out for a walk with a friend, apparently. Want to guess who the friend was?'

'Go on.'

'One Gavin Tanner. Her now-husband.'

Caroline realised she'd been holding her breath — for how long, she didn't know — and she exhaled heavily.

'Christ. So that's *twice* he's been her alibi when people around her have died?'

'So it seems.'

Caroline clenched her jaw. 'I really hate to ask this, Sara, but have you looked into the circumstances surrounding her dad's death?'

'I'm starting to now. He'd been ill for some time, I know that. There's nothing to indicate foul play, but I'll definitely be following that up in more detail after this little discovery.'

Caroline sat down and rubbed her face. 'What does your gut say, Sara? Are we looking at some sort of black widow here?'

'I honestly don't know. But you're right. Something doesn't quite sit properly, does it? It seems like too much of a coincidence.'

'I know. There goes any chance I had of sleeping tonight. Brilliant work, though, Sara. Seriously. Well done. It's probably best you go home and get some kip, though. Won't do you any good to be tired tomorrow. I've a feeling it's going to be a big day.'

'Maybe. I don't need much sleep, to be honest. If I'm going to be sitting on my own back at the flat, I might as well sit on my own here and be of some use to someone.'

Caroline looked at her and gave a sympathetic smile. 'Is there no-one special in your life? Sorry, I know I shouldn't ask. In fact, I should probably already know. I don't think it makes me a great boss either way.'

Sara smiled back, but it was a smile tinged with

sadness. 'You're fine. And no, no-one special. Not anyone that knows it, anyway.'

Caroline cocked her head slightly. She'd had her suspicions in the past, but it wasn't anything that had ever been spoken. 'Are we talking about who I think we're talking about?'

'That depends on who you think we're talking about,' Sara answered with a coy smile.

'Is the secret beau one Detective Constable Chilcott, by any chance?'

Sara's unspoken response told Caroline she was absolutely correct. She'd long suspected Aidan had been keen on Sara, but it had come as a surprise to discover it was the other way round.

'You won't say anything, will you?' Sara asked.

'To Aidan? No, of course not. It's not my place to do so. Anyway, what would I say? I'm not exactly going to go running up to him tomorrow morning, singing "Sara and Aidan, sitting in a tree, K.I.S.S.I.N.G." am I?'

Sara laughed. 'No, what I mean is I don't think he's interested. I don't think I'm his type.'

Caroline gave a disapproving look. 'Oh, I don't know about that. It probably hasn't even crossed his mind. That's no bad thing, though.'

'Mmm. Maybe.'

'Listen, you get yourself off home and get some sleep,' Caroline replied, standing up, her mind drifting back to the investigation. 'Tomorrow's going to be a big day.'

23

The next morning, Caroline arrived at work having had very little sleep. Despite her exhaustion, she just couldn't slow her brain down enough to drift off properly. In any case, the excitement of new leads and a potential breakthrough on Operation Cruickshank had provided her with enough energy to carry on.

Sara had already been in the office a couple of hours by the time Caroline got there. Caroline would've assumed she'd never left, were it not for the fact she was wearing different clothes.

'What else have we got?' Caroline asked her, eager to hear the latest.

'Not much. Just detail. Police records show there was suspicion in the case of Russell Speakman's death and that Amie Tanner was spoken to in connection with it, but that no further action was taken. She had an alibi, no apparent motive and there wasn't anything that linked her strongly enough to what'd happened. Amie and Russell didn't live together, but she was a frequent visitor. There were reports that neighbours heard them arguing earlier on the day he died, but then there's nothing until his body was discovered the following day.'

'Who found him?' Caroline asked.

'His mum. She'd popped round with a Sunday roast. Something she did each week, apparently. When he didn't answer the door, she looked through the letterbox and found him in a crumpled heap at the bottom of the stairs.'

'Wow. Happy Sunday. Are there any notes on how Amie behaved? Was she as awkward and obstinate back then too?'

'Not at first, although it seems the officers who spoke to her at the time rubbed her up the wrong way, because there are mentions later on that she started to become uncooperative. By then it was apparent they had no real evidence anyway, so it was irrelevant.'

Caroline nodded. 'Right. Good stuff, Sara. Let's get our ducks in a row, then we'll get her brought in for questioning. And this time we'll do it properly.'

It was clear that Amie Tanner was less than pleased at having been arrested and brought in for an official interview under caution. There were two types of people: those who started talking at this point because they knew things were getting serious, and those who seemed to take it as a personal affront and doubled down on their obstinacy. It looked very much like Amie Tanner was going to be in the latter camp.

She'd chosen to be accompanied by a solicitor, presumably because she was at least wise enough to realise that an interview under caution was a far more serious matter than a casual chat in one's own kitchen.

'Okay, Amie,' Caroline said as the interview began, Dexter sat beside her. 'We've been doing a bit of research and investigation at our end, as you might imagine. Does the name Russell Speakman mean anything to you?'

Amie stayed silent for a moment, briefly glancing at her solicitor, who made a non-committal gesture. 'Yes. I used to know him. Fifteen or so years ago, it will've been.'

Caroline nodded. Amie had very little choice but to answer that question. There was no way she was going to get away with claiming she didn't know Russell, and the predictable "no comment" wouldn't have held much sway in keeping the police off her back. It wouldn't look great in court, either. 'What was your relationship with Russell?' Caroline asked.

'We went out for a bit.'

'Was it serious?'

'Not especially. It only lasted two or three months.'

'I see. And what caused the relationship to end?'

Amie sighed. 'You know the answer to that, or you wouldn't have called me in here. Russell died. It was a tragic accident, but your lot were hell bent on sending someone down for it. You failed. You failed, because there wasn't anyone at fault. It was an accident. The coroner confirmed it. I was brought in by the police and interviewed, as you'll know from your records. And you'll be able to see from your records that I was released without charge because I didn't do anything wrong. And now — fifteen bloody years later — someone else I know happens to have died, and apparently I'm Dr Death or something because I suddenly become number one suspect every time someone within ten miles pops their clogs.'

'Okay. Well I think we need to calm down a little bit, Amie. We just want to get to the bottom of things. We need to determine the facts. And the facts, as I understand them, are that you were released without charge fifteen years ago because you had an alibi, is that correct?'

Amie looked at her. 'Yes.'

'And can you tell me who that alibi was?'

Amie sighed and shook her head, knowing this would all be on record already. 'Yes, it was Gavin. My husband.'

'Or your friend, as he was then.'

'Yes. We got together a little while after Russell died. He was very supportive and helpful. These things happen.'

'The same Gavin Tanner who was your alibi on the night Martin Forbes died.'

'Yes. He's my husband. We live together. Who else do you think is going to be able to say where I was? The Sultan of sodding Brunei?'

'Amie, let's calm it down. These are simple, straightforward questions. All we're trying to do is establish the facts.

There's really no need to get worked up. If everything is as you say it is, nothing's going to be a problem.'

'Well it is a problem, isn't it? Three times you've spoken to me now. And why? Because I had one poxy argument with Martin and someone I knew fifteen years ago fell down the stairs. There's literally nothing else, is there?' Amie looked at Caroline, who didn't say a word. 'Exactly what I thought. I thought you people were meant to rely on forensics and DNA and things like that, not bloody hunches.'

'All of that is being looked at as well,' Caroline said, shuffling uncomfortably in her seat, 'but these things take time, and if we get some intelligence or information early on in the investigation which we think needs following up, we're absolutely entitled to do so.'

Amie snorted. 'Intelligence. Don't make me laugh.'

Caroline cocked her head slightly. 'Amie, you're being very aggressive. All we're trying to do is ask you some simple questions and establish the facts.'

'With respect,' the solicitor said, having stayed silent until then, 'you've placed Mrs Tanner under formal caution, even though she's spoken to you quite willingly and voluntarily twice this week already. I don't believe she's refused to speak to you at any point, has she?'

'Not that I'm aware of, no,' Caroline replied.

'Then I'm glad we agree the formal caution was unnecessarily heavy handed. There was no evidence of any wrongdoing or involvement the first two times you spoke to Mrs Tanner, and as I see it the only thing that's changed is the discovery that a friend of hers died fifteen years ago. A death which the coroner declared was accidental and in which no crime was involved, I might add.'

Caroline felt her jaw tensing as she gritted her teeth. The decision to bring Amie in under caution had been potentially risky, and it hadn't paid off. Her hope had been that it might scare her into talking or revealing more than she otherwise would have, but as Caroline looked at her across the interview room table, all she saw was a far more determined steel in Amie's eyes. In that moment, she knew she'd made a big mistake.

24

FIFTEEN YEARS EARLIER

The air always felt different when she was around. Lighter, somehow. Although today it was anything but. She was usually so much fun, so friendly and bubbly. He'd never seen this side of her before, and he wasn't sure he liked it much.

Russell knew he was no angel, but he always tried to do the right thing — even if it meant failing more often than not. Of course, everyone had their weaknesses…

He could tell she was upset about something. It was clearly something he'd done, too. Surely she hadn't found out about… No, there was no way. He'd been careful. In any case, what worried him most was the silence. There was never silence when she was around. There were giggles and infectious laughter. That, amongst other things, was what appealed most about her. But today she just sat there, staring at the television, in a world of her own. It wasn't like her. In a way, it would've scared him less if she'd gone off on a rant or at least vented what was on her mind. But she was silent. And he didn't like it.

He asks her if something's wrong.

She tells him she's fine.

He says she doesn't look fine.

She asks him what that's meant to mean.

He says it wasn't meant to mean anything. He's just worried about her. She doesn't seem herself.

She makes a comment. He doesn't hear it properly, but he doesn't ask her to repeat it. He's pretty sure it wasn't something he wanted to hear anyway.

He tells her he's had enough of this. He's off for a piss. He stands and walks towards the stairs.

She doesn't like this.

He hears her pacing across the wooden floor towards him.

She explodes. She tells him she knows what he's been up to. She knows he's been shagging someone else.

He tells her that's ridiculous. Of course he hasn't. He's halfway up the stairs.

She's at the bottom. She says she's got proof. Her friend saw him kissing someone outside Ford's.

He tells her he's never heard anything so stupid in all his life. If he was going to play around, he wouldn't do it in the middle of Oakham town centre, would he? He tells her she needs to listen to herself.

She starts to head up the stairs, tells him to man up and admit it. Layla doesn't lie. She wouldn't do that. She's her best friend. She knows what she saw.

He points out that Layla never liked him anyway. Of course she's making things up to try and cause problems. She knows what Layla's like.

She says yes, she does. And she knows she can trust her. Just like she knows he's lying through his arse and he's a cheating scumbag.

He tells her to piss off out of his house if she doesn't like it.

She's at the top of the stairs. She tells him to look her in the eyes and tell her he hasn't been cheating.

He looks at her and scoffs. He tells her she's mental and he wants her to leave.

She says she's not going anywhere until she hears the truth.

He steps into the bathroom and tries to close the door.

She stands in the doorway, pushing against it.

There's a scuffle. He pushes her arm. She pushes back.

She kicks the door.

He yanks it fully open and tells her to piss off home.

She says she's not going anywhere. He's lying and she's going to prove it. She heads for his bedroom.

As she crosses the top of the stairs, he marches towards her, trying to stop her. He puts his hand on her arm.

She spins round, her fist connecting with the side of his head.

For a brief moment, their eyes meet. Before he realises what's happening, there's the briefest taste of blood — an irony tang — before he feels himself falling.

25

Caroline took a few minutes to collect her thoughts by the coffee machine before heading back to the incident room and convening a team briefing. She could tell from the way Aidan and Sara looked at her that Dexter had already told them the interview had been a disaster. One of the downsides to a small team was that bad news travelled quickly.

'Okay,' she said, raising her voice to make it clear the briefing had begun. 'Dexter and I have just conducted another interview with Amie Tanner following the discovery that a previous boyfriend of hers, Russell Speakman, died under suspicious circumstances just over fifteen years ago. It would be fair to say it didn't go brilliantly. I think for now we need to take a step back, keep our powder dry and await more concrete evidence. It'll be there, one way or the other. We're still waiting for forensics, are we, Aidan?'

'Yep. Due to hear back shortly, but nothing of note yet.'

Caroline looked at him as he spoke. She could tell something wasn't quite right. He seemed vacant somehow. 'Okay, let me know the second we hear anything back. In the meantime, I want to make it clear that Amie and Gavin Tanner are still of great interest to us. He's been her alibi twice when people close to her have died under suspicious circumstances. And yes, that's all it is for now. Circumstantial. And that's exactly why we keep digging. Sara, you've done brilliantly uncovering what you have so far, so keep on that. We need to look especially at what happened to her dad. We know he died quite young. Is there anyone else? Any other ex-boyfriends, friends, colleagues, contacts? Let's trace as much of her life as we can and speak to as many people as we can. Circumstantial evidence won't help us in court, but it could lead us towards some hard, solid evidence which will.'

'On that,' Sara said, flicking to the right page in her notebook, 'I don't think we're going to find anything suspicious when it comes to her dad's death. He'd been ill for some time and died in a hospice. And by all accounts her dad doted on her and he was the most important thing in her life, so my instinct is we're on dodgy ground with that one.'

'Alright. As I say, we'll keep digging anyway. Carefully and respectfully. Dex, can you chip in and see what else we can uncover about the death of Russell Speakman? I want to review the full coroner's report. Transcripts from the hearing, if we can. Find out who the coroner was, who did the post-mortem, who investigated the incident. I want to speak to them all. It's entirely possible there are methods available now which weren't fifteen years ago, and that we might be able to get some answers. If it was accidental, fine. If more than a few people had suspicions otherwise, that's going to need investigating.'

'Cool,' Dexter said, nodding. 'I'll get onto that. Should all be fairly simple to find out.'

'Great. Now listen, everyone. You're doing brilliantly. I know we're understaffed and under-resourced, but you're pulling out all the stops and going well beyond what's expected, and I can't ask much more than that. We've not had EMSOU on the phone trying to take over the case and even the Chief Super's been quiet, so let's crack on and make sure things stay that way, alright? The last thing we need now is for bureaucracy to get in the way.'

26

At the close of the team briefing, Caroline noticed Aidan heading towards the kitchenette and followed him.

'Aidan, can I have a quick word?' she asked.

'Sure.'

'I just wanted to check everything's okay. You seem a bit down today and I'm worried about you.'

Aidan seemed to consider this for a moment before answering. 'It's fine, honestly. It's nothing.'

'Well it's clearly something. Look, we're a small team. I care about you all. If something's on your mind, I want to help.'

'I know. I appreciate that. But you don't need to worry. It's not work related.'

'It doesn't need to be. I'm talking as your friend, not your boss. I'm concerned, that's all.'

Aidan looked at her and let out a sigh. 'I just had some bad news, that's all. A bit of a shock.'

'Nothing serious, I hope?'

'No-one's died, if that's what you mean. It's just... I've been seeing this guy for a while, and I thought things were looking really promising but he decided to let me know last night he's going to Australia for work. An offer he can't refuse, apparently. Which made me feel brilliant.'

'Ah,' Caroline said, not quite sure of the right words. She knew it was terrible to be so pre-occupied with it, but the biggest surprise for her had been the boyfriend bit.

'Sorry, you probably didn't need to know that,' he said.

'No, it's fine. I mean, of course it is. I just didn't realise... You know.'

'I don't tend to talk about my private life at work, so if you could keep all that to yourself...'

'Of course. No, of course. I wouldn't dream of telling anyone. So what are you going to do?'

Aidan shrugged. 'What can I do? I'm not moving to bloody Melbourne. Not after the way he acted. I mean, you'd think he might at least tell me he'd been offered a job and was thinking about it, wouldn't you? Or given it some thought, perhaps? But no, the first thing he tells me is he's flying out next Wednesday. Doesn't even seem to have been a hard decision for him. So if that's the way he feels, sod him. Plenty more fish in the sea and all that.'

'Well, that's a very refreshing outlook.'

Aidan shrugged again. 'Not much choice, really. I'm crap at being single. Nothing else to do but get back on the horse and find someone else.' He stopped talking as they heard footsteps approaching.

Caroline tried not to look awkward and guilty as Sara said hello and flashed an extra smile at Aidan. The poor girl. She'd been down enough, thinking that Aidan wasn't attracted to her. It'd break her heart to find out he never would be. Caroline felt awful at how quickly her worries shifted to more practical ones. They were only a small team. To have two of them living with their heads in the clouds and their hearts in the gutter would be less than ideal. But how could she possibly tell Sara there was no chance of Aidan ever being interested in her?

She forced a smile, realising and accepting — however harsh it sounded — that it simply wasn't her problem. She was more than happy to be a friend and confidante, but they were at work and she wasn't employed as an agony aunt. In any case, she had problems of her own to attend to.

27

Amie let out a deep sigh and stared at the ceiling. It wasn't the first time. She felt sure it wasn't even the hundredth time. There was little else to do in her cell other than sigh and stare.

Her solicitor had assured her she had very little to worry about, and that the police were just fishing. She wanted to believe him — she desperately wanted to trust every word — but she was starting to feel sure that she'd been deliberately set up.

After all, it wasn't the first time. The same had happened when Russell died. If she was honest with herself, she still struggled to get over that. Even the coroner's report said it had been an accident. She could still recall the interview room, the way the officers had looked at her. It was almost as if she were a zoo exhibit rather than a human being. She'd been young. Impressionable. And it had given her a deep distrust of the police.

The moment she'd heard Martin had been found dead and the police were investigating it as suspicious, she knew what would happen next. She had no reason to be worried, of course. She hadn't seen Martin for days, and she couldn't remember the last time she'd been anywhere near the viaduct. So why had she been brought in? She'd asked herself these questions a hundred times since she'd been put in this cell.

Surely it hadn't been purely down to the argument? People argued at work all the time. And yes, she'd been suspected of murder in the past, but surely the police could see it had been deemed an accident and that she had nothing to do with it? Whichever way she looked at things, all she could see was the police trying to pin something on her. It was ridiculous, especially as it had been Monique who'd been leading Martin on for so long.

They'd mentioned Gavin having been her alibi on both occasions. Of course he had! He'd been the friend she'd gone to after walking out on Russell, and they'd later married. Who else was she going to be with on a Monday evening? The whole thing was ridiculous. But she couldn't shake that nagging worry…

They had no evidence. Of course they didn't. There wasn't any. At least, not any *real* evidence. But if someone was going out of their way to make it look as though she'd done it, would they have gone as far as to fabricate something? She didn't know how, but the possibility worried her.

She'd wanted to tell her solicitor her concerns. He'd

asked her for her account and had seemed happy enough with her explanation. He seemed to believe her. He'd asked her twice whether she thought there'd be any evidence to the contrary, or anything he should be aware of, and twice she'd said no. Both times, she'd been on the verge of telling him she was worried someone might have deliberately planted evidence, but there seemed to be no right way to word it. There wasn't anyone she could suspect of doing that. She hadn't made any enemies. Mentioning it at that point would just make her sound paranoid. Suspicious, even. So she'd kept quiet.

Her solicitor had told her he didn't think she'd be kept beyond the standard twenty-four-hour custody period. Apparently the police could apply for extensions to that if they had reason to, but he thought her arrest was speculative and the evidence too spurious to get authorisation for that.

As she turned these thoughts over in her mind for the thousandth time, she heard the sound of her cell door unlocking. A young male officer looked at her and asked her to follow him.

They made their way to the custody desk, where the sergeant told her she was being released on bail without charge.

'So I'm free to go?' she asked.

'Yes and no,' the sergeant replied. 'You're being released on bail under Part 4 of the Police and Criminal Evidence Act 1984. It means we'll be continuing our investigation and that you're still under suspicion, but you won't be detained here. There are conditions for your bail, though. You'll have to remain in the country and surrender your passport until the end of the bail period, and must remain at your home address overnight. You'll be asked to report here once every seven days until the end of your bail period.'

Amie was desperately trying to listen, trying to understand everything, but all she could think of was getting out of here, getting home and seeing Gavin and the kids. Anything else could be dealt with later.

'Do you understand everything?' the sergeant asked.

Amie nodded. 'Yes. Yeah, that's fine. Thank you.'

'Would you like to call someone to come and pick you up?'

She thought for a moment, but couldn't override the deep uneasy feeling that had settled in her gut. Yes, she was going to need a lift back to Market Overton. And she knew exactly who she should call. It would be Gavin. Obviously Gavin. So why did she feel so uneasy?

28

He stared intently at the rear-view mirror and watched as Amie perched against the wall at the front entrance to Oakham Police Station.

He'd picked the perfect spot. The parking bay on Station Road meant he could watch her in his mirrors and there was no way she'd be able to see his face. She wouldn't recognise the hire car, either. She never did. His positioning gave him the best chance of getting away quickly, should he need to, but he got the impression that wouldn't be necessary.

She looked different. Her soul seemed heavier. Burdened. It wasn't the same kindly soul he'd known for all those years, loved for all those years. He could see what this had done to her, and it ate him up inside.

He hadn't wanted it to work out like this. Of course he hadn't. She was never meant to be a suspect. He'd allowed everything to get too close to home. And now he'd had to take risks in order to protect her. He knew what that meant. He knew the consequences.

He'd have to tread carefully — far more carefully than he had until now. It might not be long before they'd worked out it wasn't Amie who'd killed Martin. Not long before they worked out it had been him. He didn't know what he'd do at that point. He hadn't thought it through that carefully. But he knew he needed to. He had to have a plan. An escape route.

Everything he'd ever done had been for her. Seeing her happy, angry, upset — it had all given him ultimate clarity on what he'd needed to do at every stage. Seeing her face, how things affected her, always led him towards the right decision. And he knew that would be the case now, too.

She flicked her hair from her face, almost nonchalantly. Anyone else watching would see a woman casually waiting for a lift. But he saw so much more. He knew her better than anybody. He knew her ways, her mannerisms. He knew when they had added weight.

He didn't want her to feel like this. If only he could take her pain away… Still, he had a feeling things were going to turn out just fine in the end. After all, the new cogs were starting to turn.

29

Caroline had been keen to make amends. She knew it wasn't Mark's fault. He was trying to do his best in difficult circumstances, but it wasn't as if things were much easier for her.

At times she felt smothered, as if she didn't have the mental space to recover because he was always *there*. But there was no denying that in other senses they'd drifted. They hadn't had sex for weeks. Months, perhaps. Immediately after the hysterectomy, it had been impossible. But she felt as if Mark now looked at her in a different way when it came to sex.

It had played into all her biggest fears: that she'd feel less of a woman, that he'd resent her for not being able to bear more children. She knew that chemotherapy and major surgery hadn't done wonders for her appearance, but she hadn't expected the taps to completely switch off when it came to physical attraction.

Regardless, she was determined to fix those issues. Whatever else life threw at her, she'd never once lost her determination. Not yet, anyway.

She'd spent over an hour getting ready, and had picked out a dress she hadn't worn in a while, but which she knew Mark loved. He used to go crazy for her when she wore it, and she smiled at the memories as they came back.

After Archie and Josh were in bed, Mark went out to pick up a takeaway from Orbis in Oakham, and Caroline slipped into the dress. She knew it'd be a nice surprise for him when he got home. She went downstairs and picked out two bottles of red wine they'd had on the rack for some time. They'd been expensive, although she couldn't remember how much. She opened one of the bottles and poured two glasses, before putting them on the dining table and turning the lights down a little.

A couple of minutes later, Caroline heard the car pull up on the drive, so she headed into the kitchen to wait for Mark.

'That's an old one,' he said, gesturing at her dress as he walked in. 'Haven't seen that one for a while.'

'Oh. I thought you liked it,' Caroline replied.

Mark paused for a moment. 'I do. You know I do.'

It sounded to her as if he'd said that to placate her rather than because he actually meant it. She watched as he put the carrier bag down on the table and started to take packages of food out. 'Do you want a drink?' she asked.

'Yeah, can do.'

'Wine?'

'I'll have a beer if there's one in the fridge.'

'I opened some wine. The nice one.'

Mark looked at her. 'You mean the expensive one.'

'If you like. Who cares? I thought we might be able to make a nice night of it. It's been a while.'

Mark raised one corner of his mouth in a sympathetic smile. 'I know. I'm sorry. It's a good idea. I like it. I like the wine. It's fine. I like the dress. Love the dress. Bloody love the dress.'

Caroline laughed. 'Shut up and dish up.'

Once the food was finished and the dishes cleared away, Caroline sat down next to Mark on the sofa in the living room, a little closer than usual. More often than not they sat on completely different sofas, but tonight she'd pulled up close, draping one leg over his as she nestled her head into his shoulder.

There was nothing much on TV — a few comedy panel shows, but that didn't matter. Winding down was the main thing.

She didn't know when, but she must have dozed off for a bit, as she woke with a start when Mark switched off the TV and shuffled in his seat.

'Alright?' he asked.

'Yeah. We heading up?' she replied, sensing that he hadn't even realised she'd fallen asleep.

Mark leaned in towards her. 'Unless you were planning on doing it down here.'

She kissed him, feeling his hands on her. It'd been so long. Before Christmas. Before the—

'What's wrong?' Mark asked.

'Nothing. Let's go upstairs.'

'You were pulling away from me.'

'I wasn't.'

'You were.'

'No, I wasn't. It's just…'

'It's alright. I get it. I'm no use in that department now.'

'That's not true! Look, this is hard for both of us. We knew it would be.'

Mark nodded. 'Mmmm. Okay. Well I'm off to bed.'

30

On any other morning, a leisurely walk around one of Britain's most loved and best-known gardens would've sounded like a great idea, but Caroline barely had the energy to get out of bed. She looked at the icy blue sky through the window and considered that the bitterly cold morning might at least help wake her up.

The black roses she saw at Amie Tanner's house had played on her mind ever since she'd spotted them. When Amie had said she'd always presumed her mother or husband was sending them after her father's death, but that they had always denied this, Caroline noticed a look on Amie's face that perturbed her. It was as if Amie herself was confused by the situation, but still grateful for the memory of her dad.

Coupled with Amie's father having worked at Barnsdale Gardens in the years leading up to his death, it seemed a logical place to visit for potential information. And, if nothing else, it might help clear her mind.

She'd arranged to meet Jon Brocklebank, the Head Gardener, who'd agreed to have a chat with her. She'd already discovered from her own research that Barnsdale had been created by Geoff Hamilton, a former presenter of the television programme *Gardeners' World*, and that Barnsdale had been the official *Gardeners' World* garden for many years, until Hamilton's death.

She was pleased to find Jon waiting for her at the ticket office, smiling and ageless in only the way someone who spends their life outdoors can look. Although she didn't know the first thing about gardening, she'd been sorely tempted on many occasions to jack the job in and take to the soil. She couldn't deny there was a certain romance about it.

'Blimey. Quite a big site, isn't it?' Caroline said as Jon took her on a short guided tour.

'Yep, eight acres. We've actually managed to pack thirty-eight gardens in here, would you believe.'

'Wow. I struggle keeping up with my tiny garden. I can't imagine having to look after something like this. Especially considering its history. Must be quite daunting.'

'Ah, I'm used to it. I see you've been doing your research, though.'

'Naturally,' Caroline replied, smiling. 'Geoff Hamilton. I remember him from the telly.'

'Yes, he was very popular. One of his protégés is a presenter on *Gardeners' World* now, actually. Adam Frost.'

'Never heard of him. I guess that means you're next in line for the telly job, then, does it?'

Jon smiled and chuckled. 'I'm not sure that rule's set in stone, if I'm honest with you. But anyway, how can I help?'

Caroline took a deep breath, feeling the chill morning air coating her lungs. 'Well, it's about roses. A rose called Black Baccara, to be specific.'

'Okay. I hope you're not going to ask if you can see one, because I might have to ask you to come back in a few months,' Jon said, smiling.

Caroline chuckled. 'No, not quite. Although that does lead me on nicely to what I wanted to ask. I mean, I know roses bloom in summer, but there must be a way of having them bloom in winter. I'm thinking Valentine's Day, things like that. You see them in cut displays all year round. How do they do that?'

'Well, they'd either be imported from abroad where the flowers are already in bloom, or they'd be "forced", as it's known in the horticultural world.'

'What does that mean?' Caroline asked.

'Essentially, forcing the plants into flower by tricking them into thinking it's a different time of year. It's all about controlling warmth, adding artificial light and so on. It's much more scientific than that, but those are the basics.'

'I see. And would that be done locally?'

'It could be, but probably not. Most cut flowers in the UK tend to come from Holland. There are producers in the UK who force roses on for shows and events, but I don't know if it's year-round. And, in any case, I presume you're specifically referring to Black Bacarra?'

'Ideally, yes. The long and short of it is we need to find out where someone might have sourced them to get them into a vase in Rutland in February. Each February, in fact.'

Jon cocked his head slightly and raised his eyebrows. 'Well, it's possible someone could be growing their own if it's on a small scale. It's expensive and hard work to set up. You'd need sodium lighting and all sorts of heating apparatus. But that would be the least traceable way of doing it, presuming this is connected with some sort of crime. Otherwise, I'm almost certain there'll be commercial nurseries online who'd be happy to supply. Sorry — it's not really my area of expertise.'

'No, no that's great,' Caroline said, admiring the beauty of her surroundings. 'This is extraordinary,' she said.

'Ah, this is the Geoff Hamilton Winter Border. Named after the great man himself. He designed it specifically for winter interest, and it was redeveloped a few years ago.'

'Wow. I didn't realise there was that much you could do with a garden in winter.'

'Oh, always. It's not all about cut flowers,' Jon replied, smiling.

'No, indeed.'

'So, is there anything else I can help you with at all?'

'There is one thing,' Caroline said, her voice low. 'But

you'll have to promise never to breathe a word to any of my colleagues.'

'Erm. Okay. How can I help?' Jon gave Caroline an awkward look as she leaned in conspiratorially.

'How do I become a member?'

31

A few minutes after Caroline arrived at the station, she had convened the morning briefing. She updated the team on what she'd learnt at Barnsdale.

'In short, we're probably best off contacting commercial growers and online retailers who stock Black Bacarra for a list of anyone who's bought them over the past few years. If they're local to us or a familiar name, we've got a lead. It might be nothing. But something about it doesn't quite sit right. She knows it's not her mum or husband sending the flowers each year. And it's clearly not her dad. It might go nowhere, but it won't take up much time finding out.'

'Apart from the amount of time it takes the companies to get back to us,' Dexter said.

'That's fine. That's not on our timesheets. We've got plenty to be getting on with in the meantime. Which reminds me. We've had a few bits back. Perhaps most crucial are the preliminary DNA and forensics results as well as the post-mortem report, which, as expected after waiting around for a couple of days, have all come in at once. On the plus side, it does help us build up a picture of what happened to Martin Forbes.

'The post-mortem is strangely conclusive and inconclusive at the same time. It states there were signs of hypothermia, but that it probably wasn't the cold itself that killed him. Their conclusion on that front is that it's likely he bled out from the head wound and haemorrhaged following damage to his cranium. That's the skull, Dexter,' she said, listening as a rumble of laughter rolled through the room. 'Having said that, they note the cold would've made his heart pump harder and faster, accelerating his blood loss. Likewise, the blood loss would've had a similar effect both on itself and in lowering his body temperature. Basically, with the two combined, he stood no chance. As for the head wound, we're looking at blunt force. Forensics think it was probably a baseball bat or similar. Now, it's not easy to conceal a baseball bat, so it's likely our killer took Martin by surprise. There aren't any signs of a struggle — no skin under the fingernails or anything — but there's evidence the killer tried to strangle him, although that wasn't the cause of death. Reading between the lines, I think the head trauma knocked Martin out, the killer either believed the strangulation had worked because Martin's breathing and heartbeat had got so shallow as to be undetectable, or they simply realised there was no need because he was bleeding profusely and was clearly on his way out.'

'But there wasn't a huge amount of blood found at the scene, right?' Sara asked.

'Correct. There was some on the wall he'd been propped up against, but that's probably from direct contact with the wound. All signs seem to indicate he was dead before he was put there. Now, there was extremely heavy rain on the night Martin died, from about eight-thirty until midnight, when the temperature dropped sharply. Anything out in the open would have easily been washed away by the time we turned up. But Martin's body was under an arch in the viaduct, and actually stayed pretty dry. We'd expect to find forensic evidence or blood spillage if there was any, so we can only conclude that there probably wasn't. That means he's been killed, then transported there. Odd, seeing as it was barely yards from his running route anyway. Could just be coincidence. But the next question has to be *where* was he killed? As I see it, there are two possibilities. First, that he was killed on or near his running route, then transported to the viaduct, which is also extremely near his running route. Or, alternatively, that he was taken from his route, transported elsewhere, killed, then brought back. The riskiest option, but you can see why someone might choose it if they thought it'd reduce the likelihood of forensic evidence being found at the scene. Both pose us major issues. If it's option one, it'll be like looking for a needle in a haystack. We're talking open, public roads, evidence washed away by heavy rain, the passing of time — I could go on. If it's option two, the kill spot could've been anywhere. But there will be forensic evidence still out there. The location of the murder. The vehicle he was transported in. We know that area's not exactly rife with CCTV to say the least, so we're limited as to what we can do to generate leads. I'm thinking of a public appeal. Has a friend been behaving out of sorts, did your uncle pop out for a couple of hours, have you seen your neighbour rinsing blood out of a Ford Mondeo — that sort of thing. Any thoughts?'

The team murmured their agreement, although they all knew a public appeal would likely open up a can of worms itself. Caroline could imagine the social media posts now: *Why haven't the police found the killer yet? Why are we doing their jobs for them? Isn't that what we pay their wages for? Too busy prosecuting innocent motorists!* It was one of the many reasons why Caroline kept off social media as a rule. It was futile trying to point out to a keyboard warrior that motoring offences — funnily enough — tended to be dealt with by road traffic units rather than murder investigation teams, and that was before she got round to mentioning that the fact they'd been prosecuted showed they weren't all that innocent after all. Regardless, the potential benefits of a public appeal would far outweigh the eye-rolling caused by gobby Facebookers.

'Just one other thing,' Dexter said. 'I checked up on the Russell Speakman investigation, to see what involvement police had at the time. I couldn't find much, but the investigating officer was DCI Bob Barrington. I don't know if he'll remember it at all, but he might. He retired shortly after, so you never know.'

'Nice one, Dex,' Caroline replied. 'Do we have contact details for him?'

'Yep. He's still local. Lives over in King's Cliffe, apparently.'

'Excellent. Be rude not to pop in and say hello, wouldn't it?'

After the briefing had concluded, Caroline headed straight for the coffee machine in the kitchenette. A moment or two later, Sara joined her.

'All okay?' Sara asked. 'You look a bit flustered.'

Caroline laughed. 'I think I look like I've been marched round Barnsdale Gardens on a freezing cold morning after spending the last couple of months in bed.'

Sara smiled. 'Actually, I was hoping I might be able to confide in you.'

'Go on.'

'It's about Aidan. He's been down recently. You've probably noticed. I'd be willing to put money on it being a relationship breakup. There's all the classic signs — looking annoyed after reading a text message, being a bit absent, clearly in a world of his own. He's definitely been dumped by a woman. I've got a bit of an instinct for things like this.'

Caroline raised her eyebrows and murmured an awkward agreement. She didn't have the heart to tell Sara how wrong her instincts were.

'But I was thinking,' Sara continued, 'about possibly

asking him out. I know it sounds ridiculous so soon after his relationship has broken up, but maybe it's what he needs. In any case, I don't really want to risk him finding someone else or getting back with his ex-girlfriend. *Carpe diem*, they say, don't they? What do you think?'

Caroline shuffled awkwardly. 'Uh. Well, I don't know. I mean, it is very soon. And of course you don't know if he'd be interested.'

'No, but I won't know for sure until I ask, will I? And I think I've noticed a few signs that he is.'

I don't think you have, Caroline wanted to say. 'How about... How about I have a word with him? Not directly, but on the quiet. Put out a few feelers. That way you'll know if it's worth pursuing.'

'Would you? Oh, that'd be amazing. Thank you.'

Caroline forced a smile. 'Don't mention it. But Sara? Just... Just wait until then, okay? I don't want you to get your hopes up. Just in case.'

'Just in case,' Sara said, winking. 'Mum's the word.'

32

It took Caroline the best part of half an hour to drive to King's Cliffe, a small village just over the border in Northamptonshire. She'd heard of it, but had never visited before. It seemed pleasant enough — a mixture of old and new buildings, most built in the local sandstone that made so much of the local area feel like home. It was a fairly compact village, but with lots of tight, winding roads which left Caroline feeling glad she had a sat-nav. She could have easily got lost amongst the narrow side-roads otherwise.

Eventually, she arrived at the home of former DCI Bob Barrington, the officer who'd been in charge of the brief investigation into Russell Speakman's death. The truth was that any sudden or unexpected deaths outside of a hospital required police intervention of some sort, even if only to quickly determine all was fine and things could be handed over to the undertakers. In some cases, that involvement lasted a little longer.

Once pleasantries had been exchanged and coffee had been poured, they sat down in Barrington's living room and Caroline explained the reason for her visit.

'We're investigating a case which we believe might have links to a job you worked on fifteen years ago,' she said. 'I think it's one of those where there's not enough to go on in either case, but put the two together...'

'I see where you are,' Barrington replied. 'So how can I help?'

'Do you remember investigating the death of a Russell Speakman in Oakham?'

A flicker of recognition crossed Barrington's face. 'Speakman. Yes, fell down the stairs, didn't he? I remember it well. Something not right about that. You're onto something. What's the current case?'

'A murder.'

'Not that one over at the viaduct?' Barrington asked, his head cocked.

'That's the one.'

Barrington nodded. 'I see. Got herself a new chap, did she?'

'Who?' Caroline asked, trying to sound as clueless and innocent as possible.

'Christ, I can't remember her name. Murray, was it?'

'Amie Murray?'

'That's the one. Speakman's girlfriend. One of, anyway.'

'Yes. She's married now.'

'To your new stiff, I presume?'

'No. No, that's the thing. There's some suggestion that the victim was interested in her, but she claims it wasn't reciprocated. By all accounts, she wasn't particularly keen on him.'

Barrington raised an eyebrow. 'I see. Well I probably shouldn't be asking you the questions. Old habits, and all that. It's probably best I tell you what I recall, and you can see what's of interest.'

'Okay.'

Barrington shuffled in his chair, as if it would help bring memories to the forefront. 'So, call comes in. There's a body. Likely accidental, but assistance required. If I remember rightly it was called in by Speakman's mum. Uniform attend, and one of them gets the sense something isn't right. This is a young man, sober, who's somehow fallen backwards down the stairs and died. Extremely uncommon, to say the least. So I get the call. And I've got to say, I'm in agreement. It seems odd. We ask around, pull a few strings and find out more about Speakman. He's a bit of a dosser, bit of a lad, but never been in any trouble. Closest he gets is shagging about a bit, but that's hardly uncommon. But the girlfriend's name comes up. Murray.'

'Amie Murray.'

'That's it. Neighbours heard them having an almighty row the day before and she stormed out. Said it wasn't a particularly rare occurrence, and that she wasn't the only woman he had coming and going. Now, that raised alarm bells, see. Are we talking about a jealous lover here? I think possibly so. So we look into it a bit further. Speak to people. She's got anger issues. So we bring her in for questioning. Trouble is, we've got nothing we can pin on her. Her DNA's obviously all over his house because she's his girlfriend. One of them, anyway. There's a strong suspicion Speakman didn't just fall and was pushed, but it's not strong enough to prove it, and definitely not strong enough to prove *who* did it. In any case, she's got an alibi. She went straight from Speakman's to a friend's house, and they went out for a walk, got some food and various other bits that evening, then she stayed the night. Pathologist reckoned Speakman had died later on, probably in the evening, so he was alive when she left his. That's what stopped it dead, so to speak. At the time Speakman died, she had an alibi, and a pretty bloody solid one at that, as far as we were concerned.'

Caroline nodded. 'But your suspicions remained?'

'Yep. Not much you can do with suspicions, though, when you're struggling for evidence. And you think she might be connected with this new murder? The Murray girl, I mean.'

'Amie? Yes. She's Amie Tanner now, though.'

Barrington's face turned grey in front of her. 'Sorry, did you say Tanner?'

'That's her married name, yes.'

'Jesus Christ. What's the husband's name? Gary, isn't it?'

'Gavin. Do you know him?'

'Christ, do I. He was her alibi when Speakman died, did you know that?'

'Yeah. We did. That's what makes me wonder if there's a connection somewhere.'

Barrington let out a noise that sounded like a football hitting a bush. 'You can say that again. Gavin Tanner's "connections" are exactly what scuppered our investigation last time.'

Caroline cocked her head slightly. 'How do you mean?'

Barrington looked at her. 'Christ. You really don't know, do you?'

Caroline felt her heart starting to beat more heavily in her chest. 'Know what?'

'Gavin Tanner's dad was Alf Tanner. Chief Constable Alf Tanner as he was then. We had pressure from above to close the investigation and write it off as an accidental death. Said there was no benefit to be had from spending time on it. The thing is, we didn't think for one moment Amie had gone back to Speakman's house to kill him. We were pretty certain it was Gavin Tanner.'

33

As soon as Caroline had left Bob Barrington's house, she called Chief Superintendent Derek Arnold and told him she needed to see him urgently. He was in meetings, but would be free a little later, he replied. Keen to find out more about former Chief Constable Alf Tanner, she arranged to meet Arnold in his office later that day.

In the meantime, she decided to head back to Oakham via Seaton, so she could drop in on Sandra Forbes. A specialist Family Liaison Officer had been appointed to keep the family abreast of developments and ensure they were being cared for, but it wasn't too unusual for the Senior Investigating Officer to make further direct contact. In Caroline's experience, it was common — once the initial shock had subsided — for some more organised and logical thoughts to start to come to the fore. Occasionally, memories would start to make sense and those close to the victim would have information that could be useful to the investigation.

She parked up outside Sandra Forbes's house and knocked on the door. Sandra opened it a few moments later, a look on her face that bordered hopeful and fearful.

'We don't have any major news at the moment,' Caroline said, keen not to get Sandra's hopes up too much that her husband's death had been solved. 'I was just passing by and thought I'd pop in and see how you were doing, give you a bit of an update.'

They sat down in Sandra's kitchen, which Caroline noticed was still immaculately clean. She supposed scrubbing the house from top to bottom was a relatively effective distraction from the thoughts that must have been plaguing Sandra's every waking minute.

'How're things going with the business?' Caroline asked, keen to get Sandra talking.

'Alright, I think. I've not had a chance to sit down and look at everything. It can run itself for a bit. People understand.'

'It looks like he built a good team there.'

'Mostly, yes. I tried not to get too involved.'

'Have you been in touch with any of the staff at all?'

Sandra shook her head. 'Not yet. I'm just trying to distract myself, you know? I need to stop my brain from thinking about… Thinking about *it*.'

'I understand.'

At that moment, Caroline's phone rang. 'Sorry,' she said. 'Do you mind if I take this?'

'No, of course.'

She stood up and walked out into the hallway, answering her phone. 'DI Hills.'

'Ah. Hi. It's Tom Mackintosh from Allure Design. The IT guy.'

'Hi Tom. What's up?'

'Uh, well, it's a bit delicate actually. I don't really want to discuss it on the phone, but I was hoping I might be able to meet up with you.'

Caroline looked at her watch. 'Where are you? At work?'

'Yeah.'

'Alright. I'm not too far away. I can be there in five or ten. Everything okay?'

'Honestly? I'm not sure. I think it's probably best you come and see this for yourself.'

34

A few minutes later, Caroline arrived outside the offices of Allure Design in Uppingham. She texted Tom to say she was there, and he met her at the front door. She figured it was preferable to listening to Monique reciting passages from Virgil as she signed her in.

A few moments later, they sat down in Martin Forbes's office.

'Okay,' Tom said, releasing a deep breath as he sat. 'I know your guys have got backups and mirrors and all sorts of things, but I was sorting out Martin's laptop earlier. I was hoping I could recondition it and re-use it in the company somewhere, or maybe give it to Sandra if she needs it. And I... Look, I hope I haven't broken any laws here, but you know how it is. I was there, I had access to look, and... Well...'

'You went snooping.'

'No. Not like that. Nothing illegal or anything. I mean, it's my job to handle the IT systems.'

Caroline smiled. 'Tom, it's okay. I'm joking with you. If you've found something useful, I'm all ears.'

Tom seemed to calm a little. 'Okay. Well, it's a MacBook, see? The browser saves passwords and logins so you don't need to keep remembering them and typing them in every time. Anyway, I opened the browser, and his Gmail inbox came up. It was already logged in. I mean, my first thought was to close it down and log him out, but then something caught my eye.'

'Go on.'

Tom lifted the lid of the laptop, brought it to life then pointed at the screen. 'There are emails from Gavin Tanner. Amie's husband. Sent to Martin's personal email address.'

Caroline's heart rate quickened. 'Okay. Have you read them?'

'There's only a couple. The first one is here, look.'

Caroline read the screen in front of her.

Gavin Tanner
to me

I think you and I need to have a little chat.

'Okay,' Caroline said. 'Interesting. Did Martin reply?'

'No. He'd read it, but didn't send anything back. Then Gavin emails again two days later.'

Gavin Tanner

to me

You've got two options. You can either meet me for a little chat or I'll tell your wife, your family and everybody else what's been going on.

'I was a bit surprised he put all that in writing, to be honest,' Tom said. 'I don't know what it means, but it doesn't look good.'

'No, I'm inclined to agree,' Caroline replied. 'Did Martin say anything back?'

'Yep, he replied to that one. Here you go.'

Martin Forbes

to Gavin

Not at mine, and not at work. Meet me this evening. I'll be out running anyway. Seven o'clock, just outside Seaton. Here:

Underneath the text was an image that looked as if it'd been grabbed from Google Maps. On it, Martin had marked an area near the B672, where he wanted Gavin Tanner to meet him. Caroline recognised it immediately. It was the exact spot where they'd found Martin's body.

35

Despite the crisp day and bright blue sky, it felt like a dark cloud was starting to envelope Caroline as she left Uppingham and headed back towards Oakham. She'd already called Dexter to update him on what she'd discovered, and had put out a call for Gavin Tanner's arrest. Although they were going to need far more to charge him, Tanner would soon realise the net was closing in and he would then pose a significant flight risk. With substantial evidence as to his involvement, accessing his car tracker was now very much on the cards too.

She arrived back at the station around fifteen minutes later, having had yet another close call with an oncoming car deciding to overtake three others on the A6003 just outside Manton. It was a stretch of road which always made her nervous, especially as she knew how many incidents uniformed officers regularly had to deal with round there.

She'd spent the whole drive trying to figure out how would be best to approach the situation with Chief Superintendent Arnold, but she couldn't find the words. She supposed the only real way forward was to start from the beginning. But there was a nagging thought at the back of her mind; a worry that if a former Chief Constable had potentially sabotaged an investigation to save his own son's skin, it was entirely possible other officers might have been involved.

Caroline knew Arnold had been working for the force when Alf Tanner was Chief Constable, and was hoping her superior officer might be able to shed some light on the man, but it wasn't the first time she'd thought twice about Arnold's motives. There was something about him she'd never quite been able to put her finger on. However much she thought about that, though, she had no doubt that Arnold's motives were always sound.

She knocked on his door and waited to be called in, then sat down across the desk from him.

'How're things going?' Arnold asked, seeming genuinely interested.

'Alright, I think. We're making good progress on Operation Cruickshank. I should have some more definitive news on that in the next few hours.'

'Good. I've been trying to give you plenty of breathing space on that one. I hope you noticed.'

'I did indeed. It's much appreciated. Thank you.'

Arnold nodded. 'And how's the... the health thing?'

'Fine. I feel much better, thanks for asking.'

'You sure?' Arnold asked. 'Only I know what you're like for pushing through and pretending everything's fine. If there are issues, you will need to let me know. I've got a responsibility for your welfare at work. You know that.'

'If anything changes, you'll be the first to know,' Caroline said, forcing a smile.

'Good. Now, I'm guessing this isn't a social visit?'

'No. It's a bit of an odd one, though. You've been knocking about a while, haven't you, sir?'

Arnold straightened up in his chair. 'Alright. No need to get personal.'

'I mean, you were here when Alf Tanner was Chief Constable, weren't you?'

Arnold visibly bristled at the mention of Tanner's name. 'I was, yes.'

'What was he like? Did you get along?'

The Chief Superintendent took a deep breath and straightened his tie. 'Well, I wasn't a Chief Super then. I think I was either a Sergeant or Inspector when he retired, so we didn't really have many interactions.'

Caroline got a heavy sense there was something unspoken playing on Arnold's mind. 'Was he... was he alright?' she asked.

Arnold seemed to think for a few moments before speaking, forming the right words in his head. 'He was... He was old school. One of the last, really. Things were different then. But again, this is all hearsay. I never really knew the man.'

'Just before he retired, there was a suspicious death. A

man fell down the stairs at home, but the attending officers believed he was pushed. Pretty much everyone did, from what I can tell, but nothing ever came of it.'

'Speakman,' Arnold whispered, nodding.

'You remember it?'

'Yes. I wasn't working on the case, but I heard about it. Everyone heard about it.'

'Do you remember who the main suspect was?'

'Of course I do. Why do you think I remember it? What's this all about, Caroline?'

'Alf Tanner's son, Gavin.'

Arnold shook his head. 'No. No, you've got that round your neck. His lad was the alibi for the girl they thought did it. Speakman's girl.'

Caroline looked at him. 'You really haven't kept up to speed with Operation Cruickshank, have you?'

Arnold's eyes narrowed. 'What's going on, Caroline? What's this about?'

'Do you remember her name? The suspect.'

'Can't say I do, no,' Arnold answered with a long exhalation of breath.

'Amie Murray, her name was. She's now Amie Tanner.'

'They married?'

'Oh yes. She works at the company owned by Martin Forbes, the man whose body was found under the viaduct. She and Martin had a massive row a couple of days before he died. According to colleagues, there were suspicions that something had been going on. Gavin Tanner, previously her alibi and now her husband, provided yet another alibi for her. That was dodgy enough to start alarm bells ringing, but then we found these.'

Caroline passed her phone across the desk. She'd taken photos of the emails Gavin Tanner had sent to Martin Forbes. As he read them, Arnold's face dropped.

'This is definitely his email address?' he asked.

'Yes.'

'Have you brought him in?'

'In the process of.'

Arnold sat back in his chair and rubbed his head. 'Christ. Why did those stupid old buggers always think they knew best? "This is the way it's always been done, lad. Never did us any harm." Jesus Christ. Worked out fine for them, didn't it? Course it did. Gave them an easy ride. But it's not them who's got to clear up their mess years later.'

'I've got to say, sir, this could get worse. We could be opening up a whole can of worms, here. Who's to say Alf Tanner wasn't bent from the start? Who knows what else he'd been up to?'

'Well I wouldn't worry too much about that,' Arnold said, his voice almost a whisper. 'Alf Tanner's been dead seven years.'

36

Gavin Tanner cut a steely figure as Caroline and Dexter sat opposite him in the interview room. In that moment, she could see where Amie had learnt her arrogance. They made quite the team. Always had, it seemed.

It was usually the case that bolshie suspects were reined in by their solicitors, if the solicitor wasn't the bolshie one to begin with. In this case, though, Gavin Tanner's brief looked like a man who'd just had his pants pulled down in front of the class.

'Okay, are you happy to get started?' Caroline asked them as a matter of courtesy, before initiating the recording.

'Gavin, can you talk us through your movements on the night Martin Forbes died, please?'

Gavin looked up at the ceiling and sighed, his arms crossed over his chest. 'We've been through this. Many times.'

'This is your first interview, Gavin.'

'But you haven't stopped hassling my wife, have you? She's told you every single time she was at home with me all evening, so where do you suppose I was?'

'That's what I'm asking you, Gavin.'

Gavin stared, almost glared, at Caroline. 'I. Was. At. Home.'

'All evening?'

'Yes. All evening.'

'Any witnesses other than your wife?'

'Yeah, we had a mariachi band in for the night. Fancied a bit of light entertainment. How many bloody witnesses do you think I've got? The kids were in bed, it was just us.'

'So you didn't leave the house at all? Even for a few minutes?'

Gavin leaned forward. 'What part of "all evening" didn't you understand?'

'Did you know Martin Forbes personally?'

It seemed to take a moment for Gavin to adjust to the shift in questioning. 'No. No, I didn't. He was Amie's boss. That's about all I knew of him.'

'Ever meet him?'

'Once or twice, briefly, if I popped by the office or had to pick Amie up from work or some event.'

'Did you get on?'

'We barely knew each other. I can't say I liked him or disliked him.'

'So you hadn't had any recent contact with Martin?'

'Oh for Christ's sake, how many times do you want to ask me the same bloody question in different ways? Do you think I'm just going to suddenly "slip up" and give you the opposite answer? It's ridiculous.'

'Are you an angry man by nature, Gavin?' Caroline asked.

Dexter had to force himself to cover his smile, hoping Tanner and his solicitor hadn't noticed it. It was one of Caroline's 'cornering' questions for suspects: one which had no right answer. Saying yes would potentially incriminate them, and anything else would force them to calm down and moderate their behaviour.

'You'd be angry if you were in my situation. You've been harassing my wife constantly, and now me.'

'With respect, being asked to attend a police interview isn't harassment. Nor is us interviewing you under caution. But I understand it must be quite frustrating. Especially considering your past history.'

Tanner's eyes narrowed. 'What's that meant to mean?'

'You had a similar experience about fifteen years ago, didn't you?' Caroline asked, flicking through her papers as if she'd only read a brief mention of it and wasn't fully appraised of the facts. 'Ah, yes. Here we are. Your wife — friend, as she was then — was questioned in connection with the suspicious death of a man she'd been in a relationship with. You were her alibi.'

'With respect, Detectives,' the solicitor asked, shuffling in his chair like a child saying his first lines in a school play, 'do you have anything other than coincidence?'

'Oh yes,' Caroline answered, smiling. 'Don't worry, we'll come to that. Can you talk us through what happened on the night Russell Speakman died, Gavin?'

Gavin let out a belly laugh. 'What? No, of course I bloody can't. I can barely tell you what I did three weeks ago, never mind fifteen years ago. It was a non-event.'

'You were the alibi for a woman suspected of murder. She wasn't charged, partially because of your alibi. Partially.'

'What's that meant to mean?'

'We'll come to it, I'm sure. Shall I read the statement you gave to the police at the time?'

Tanner leaned back in his chair and folded his arms again. 'Yeah, go on. Why not. I could do with a snooze.'

'Don't relax too much. It's short. But then again it didn't need to be any longer, did it? "Amie Murray arrived at my house a few minutes after two o'clock p.m. She seemed upset so we went for a walk through the fields towards Brooke. We were out for two and a half hours, then we went back to Oakham because it was going to start to get dark within the hour. We had a few drinks at the Grainstore, then went back to mine, where we both stayed until the next morning." Does that sound familiar, Gavin?'

'If you say so.'

'We know you were at the Grainstore late afternoon and early evening. The staff confirmed it at the time. But there are no witnesses to anything after you left.'

Tanner signed. 'We've been through this. It's a bit difficult to summon up witnesses when you're at home on your own. In any case, I wasn't a suspect. I didn't need an alibi. All I did was tell your lot where Amie was all night.'

'Have you always looked out for her?'

'I've always told the truth, yes. I know it might look like a bloody big coincidence from your point of view, but I'm telling you now that's all it is. So yes, obviously I'm going to be protective of her.'

'I bet she felt quite safe with you, didn't she?' Caroline asked, starting to go in for the kill.

'I hope so. That's what spouses are for.'

'I mean, what with your background and everything. I imagine she felt very... no, not safe. That's not the word I want. *Protected.*' Caroline watched as Gavin Tanner's jaw tensed. 'Do you think she felt protected, Gavin?'

'I don't know. Are you trying to insinuate something?'

'No, not at all. I just imagine she would've felt pretty secure with you wanting to look after her. Especially considering your dad was Chief Constable of Rutland Police.'

Tanner was silent for a moment. His solicitor looked like he was about five miles out of his depth. 'What's that meant to mean?' Tanner asked.

'Did your old man pull a few strings, Gavin? Don't worry, I get that Russell Speakman wasn't the nicest bloke on earth. Not by a long shot. I'd hazard a guess there were more people glad he was gone than missed him. I imagine your old man knew that as much as anyone. So what happened? She came over to yours, told you what a bastard he was, you spent a couple of hours walking and talking about how much he'd upset her, had a few drinks, then... what? Decided to go over and have it out with him?'

'For Christ's sake, this is ridiculous. You didn't have a single shred of evidence then, and you don't have one now, either. Stick me on a lie detector test. Do what you have to do. I don't care. This is all a complete waste of time.'

'I'm afraid polygraphs don't tend to be admissible in court, largely because they're nonsense,' Caroline said.

'Yeah, well that makes two things that can be described like that, doesn't it?'

Caroline forced a smile. 'We'll see, Gavin. We'll see.'

37

Caroline and Dexter left the interview room and glanced at their watches simultaneously.

'Jesus,' Dexter said. 'Hardly worth going home at this point. Might as well nip to Boots for a toothbrush.'

Caroline straightened her spine and pushed her shoulders back, feeling and hearing the vertebrae cracking as she tried to settle into some sort of skeletal comfort. 'I don't know what I'm more worried about,' she said. 'Missing out on sleep or lying down and not being able to get back up again.'

'It's your age. Us young'uns can go all night. That's not a come-on, by the way.'

Caroline laughed. 'Don't worry, Dex. I didn't think in a million years it would be.'

'We might as well call it a night,' Dexter replied, thumbing a gesture towards the interview room. 'If we keep him up any longer his brief'll want to start claiming torture through lack of sleep.'

'I know how he feels. Get custody to escort him back down the corridor to our finest luxury penthouse suite and we'll carry on in the morning.'

They headed up to the incident room to collect their things, and Caroline decided to give her email inbox one last check. She was glad she did.

'Dex. Look at this.'

Dexter walked over, his eyes red with fatigue. 'What's up?'

'We've got the data back from Gavin Tanner's car tracker. It says here it doesn't track actual journeys, only start points and end points.'

'Okay. Is that a bad thing?'

'That depends. It shows his car being started at his home at 6.23 on the evening Martin Forbes died. The next time the engine goes off, he's back at home again at 7.56pm.'

'So can we prove exactly where he went in the meantime?'

Caroline looked at the screen again, trying to work her way through the possibilities. 'That, Dex,' she said, 'is the million pound question.'

38

Back at home, Caroline found Mark waiting up for her, but the atmosphere was frostier than it needed to be. He had a wonderful way of pretending nothing had happened if he'd been the one at fault in an argument, but if it was down to something Caroline had said or done he could be in a mood for days. He always came round eventually, but Caroline wasn't interested in waiting. She wanted to iron things out, even if that meant grovelling.

'Look, I'm sorry about the other night,' she said as she sat down on the sofa. 'I know how hard you've been trying and I know it's no excuse, but what I've been through... it really messes with your body. And your mind. I just... I can't explain the things it changes.'

'Changes?'

'Not the way I feel towards you. I promise. Please, never think that. It's entirely me. It's so difficult to explain. It feels like a part of me has been taken away. I mean, it has, but you know... It makes me feel differently about myself.'

'How so?' Mark asked, his voice soft. For the first time in a long time, she felt as if he was finally listening, actually taking in what she was saying.

'I don't know,' she said, trying to put it into words. 'Less of a woman. Less attractive. Less... sexual.'

Mark nodded slowly. 'I get that. But, I mean, you were all dressed up. Made up. Candles, red wine. The expensive ones. Then after all that... I was just surprised, I suppose. I thought you wanted to.'

'I did.'

'And I'm not trying to belittle what you're going through, but for me, after all that, to have you suddenly change your mind...'

'I didn't change my mind.'

'You did.'

'No, I just realised I couldn't jump straight in with two feet and expect to immediately feel twenty-one years old again. It'll take time. Small steps.'

Mark nodded. 'Okay. Well, I'm willing to try if you are.'

'Of course I am. I have been.'

'You've been kind of cold. Distant.'

Caroline swallowed. 'I know. I've been trying up here, though,' she said, tapping her head. 'It might not seem like it from the outside, but there's a lot of work to do in there before it'll show much.'

Mark took her hand. 'I know. And I'm always here to

support you through it, alright? I just need you to tell me what you want. I can't keep guessing and getting it wrong. I need you to lead this and help me out too.'

'Okay,' Caroline replied, smiling, but unsure as to how this was going to play out. Regardless, she had hope. It had to be worth all the effort of trying. Otherwise, they had nothing. 'It's a deal,' she said.

39

There were always aspects of the job which some officers enjoyed and others didn't. For Caroline, one of the most enjoyable aspects was interviewing suspects. There was a logic to it, a tried and tested process which got results and gave her a huge amount of satisfaction.

It was, of course, frustrating at times not to be able to walk into the first interview, dump all the evidence on the table and wrap things up there and then, but the key was to let the suspect do that work for them.

The first interview was about establishing the facts, letting the suspect weave their own narrative, even if it was clearly contrary to what the officers already knew. In effect, they were giving them enough rope to hang themselves. At that point, they'd regroup and reassess, compile everything then go back in for the second interview. That was when those bombshells would be dropped. The suspect wouldn't be in a position to make up excuses and ways of wriggling out of it, because they'd already committed to a position the police could now prove was false. This was the position Caroline felt they were now in, and she was looking forward to it immensely.

'Okay, Gavin,' she said once the second interview had begun the next morning. 'In your last interview you told us a couple of things we found quite interesting, to say the least. You stated that you'd stayed at home on the night Martin Forbes died. Do you want to make any amendments to that statement?'

'No, I do not.'

'Gavin, your car has been seized and is being searched, as has the clothing you were wearing that night. Are we going to find anything there that'll incriminate you?'

Gavin didn't seem so certain in answering this question. 'I don't imagine so, no.'

'You don't imagine so? You don't sound sure.'

'Well I don't know what you're looking for, do I?'

'You must know if there's anything incriminating. If you didn't kill Martin Forbes and weren't involved in his murder, there won't be, will there?'

Gavin crossed his arms. 'Then there won't be.'

'We're also looking through your mobile phone and laptop. Do you think we'll find anything there?'

'I didn't know you'd taken my laptop,' Gavin said, his eyes narrowed.

'Oh yes. You're under arrest, Gavin. That allows us the

power to enter your property, search for evidence and remove anything we think might be of interest or value to our investigation.' Caroline watched him, trying to gauge his reaction. 'You've gone a bit quiet, Gavin. Perhaps I should ask you another question. Have you been in touch with Martin Forbes recently? In the days leading up to his death, perhaps? I know we've already asked you this, but I think it bears repeating at this point.'

Gavin's solicitor leaned in slightly towards him. 'You don't have to answer any questions you're not comfortable with.'

'No comment,' Gavin said.

'Okay. Can you have a look at these for me, please?' Caroline replied, passing two sheets of paper across the desk. 'Do you recognise them?'

'No comment.'

'They're emails. Between you and Martin Forbes. Can you tell me the date on them please?'

'No comment.'

'It was very shortly before Martin died, wasn't it?'

'No comment.'

'In these emails, Gavin, you ask Martin to meet you. He suggests Monday evening — the night he died — at the exact location where his body was found the next morning. That's the arrangement that was made. Do you have any comment on that?'

Gavin looked at his solicitor.

'You don't have to answer that.'

'I do,' Gavin said. 'I really do. Because I know where this is going, and I know how it looks. But it's not the case. Yes. Okay. I arranged to meet Martin that night. I went there. You'll probably find mud on the tyres that matches Seaton, if that's what you're looking for. But Martin didn't turn up. You have to believe me. He wasn't there. That's why I went home.'

'Why did you want to meet him?'

Gavin sighed. 'Because Amie told me about the argument they'd had. He's been trying it on with her for months. She keeps turning him down. Obviously. But she got the feeling he'd been using that to justify being an absolute arse to her ever since. He kept slagging off her work, talking down to her in front of people, calling her in for endless meetings to stop her finishing projects and then complaining that projects hadn't been finished. He basically tried to make her working life hell because she wouldn't put out for him. So yeah, I wanted to have a chat with him. I wanted to tell him it wasn't on, that I knew what'd been happening and that he needed to stop. But he didn't turn up.'

'What time did you arrive?' Caroline asked.

'Just before seven. Ten to, I think.'

'And how long did you stay?'

'Until half past. It was obvious then he wasn't going to turn up and had just pussied out of it.'

'Did you stay in your car the whole time?'

'God yes. It was cold and drizzling. I stayed inside with the heaters on.'

Caroline and Dexter exchanged a look. 'And did you see anyone else around?' Caroline said.

'No-one. A couple of cars drove past on the road, but no-one stopped. No-one on foot either, but that was hardly surprising.'

It was always a risk to change the line of questioning at a time like this, but Caroline wanted to see how he'd react. 'Did you suspect there might be something more to the relationship between Amie and Martin?' she asked. 'That maybe it wasn't just unwanted attention, but that perhaps something had been going on between them?'

Gavin's jaw tensed. That told Caroline all she needed to know. 'No,' he said. 'She's not like that. She's not that sort of woman.'

'Okay. Back to Monday night. What happened when you realised Martin hadn't turned up? Did you try to call him?'

Gavin shook his head. 'No. I don't have a number for him. I only had his personal email address because he'd sent some jokey forwarding thing to Amie a while back and she'd forwarded it on to me. But I did email him to call him a coward.'

Caroline and Dexter looked at each other again. 'When was this?' she asked.

Gavin shrugged. 'Around that time. Half seven-ish. Just before I left Seaton and came home. I was bloody fuming that he'd got me all the way out there, left me sitting in a sodding car park for over half an hour and not bothered turning up.'

Caroline jotted a note in her book, in deliberate view of Dexter. *Make sure they check G's sent items.*

'Did you definitely send that to Martin's email address?'

'Of course I did. Who else would I send it to?'

'I was just wondering, because we didn't find it in Martin's inbox. It's a bit strange that he'd delete that email but not the others, isn't it?'

Gavin shrugged again. 'I dunno. I can't answer that for him, can I? All I know is I replied to the existing thread, so there's no way it went anywhere else.'

Caroline tried to formulate her thoughts, but found she was struggling. It all seemed so clear, but at the same time completely the opposite. The evidence seemed to be growing, and there was definitely something suspicious about Gavin's behaviour. But she was doubtful there was enough for a charge. An extension awaiting further evidence and results from forensics, yes. But she was also cautious about putting too much stock in one suspect. She'd made that mistake before.

'So let's get things straight,' she said. 'You suspect that Martin has been trying it on with your wife. You tell him you want to meet and talk to him. You don't say why. You arrange to meet under the viaduct on Monday evening. You claim he never turned up and that you sent him an email calling him a coward for not turning up, but just a few hours later his body is found at that exact spot. You lied to us when you said you hadn't left the house that evening. You lied when you said you hadn't been in recent contact with Martin Forbes. And you lied when you said you didn't kill him, didn't you Gavin?'

'No! I didn't kill him. And I don't know who did, either.' He leaned forward, his elbows on the table. A mark of deliberate sincerity, whether acted or true. 'Look at this from my point of view. I arranged to meet the guy, he didn't turn up, then his body's found right where I'd been. How do you think that looks from here? I know exactly how it looks from your side of things. So yeah, of course I didn't bloody tell you I'd driven down there to meet him. And of course I didn't tell you about the emails.'

Caroline scoffed. 'Did you think we wouldn't find out?'

'No! I don't know. I just... I don't know. I thought maybe by then you'd have found who actually killed him. I guess part of me thought you'd have no real reason to suspect me because I didn't do it, so there was no way I was just going to phone up and tell you all this, was there? And then when you started sniffing round, there was nothing I could do but hang on and hope you found whoever did it first. Jesus Christ, I've got kids. A family. A job. I'm not about to kill some bloke because he fancies my wife. I mean, come on. You've seen her. He's not the first guy to try it on with her. Not by a long shot. Just think about it. This doesn't make any sense.'

'Not in isolation, no. But you've already protected Amie once, haven't you? You were her alibi when Russell Speakman died.'

'Of course I bloody was. I was with her! What else did you expect me to say? And of course I protect her. She's my wife. But I don't go murdering every bloke who looks at her, for crying out loud. What do you think I am?'

Caroline looked at Gavin, desperately trying to work out the answer to that question for herself.

40

After the interview, Caroline and Dexter sat down in her office and tried to process the fallout.

'It's bizarre,' she said. 'It's almost like there are two instincts there. There's the one that says of course he did it, he's lied about being at the scene until we proved otherwise, he lied about not even leaving the house, he lied about not being in contact with Martin, so what else is he lying about? And that's before we get onto the whole Russell Speakman thing. But then there's that other instinct you get from spending time with him, and that tells me he didn't do it.'

'He could just be very convincing,' Dexter said. 'If we're talking genuine psychopathy or something along those lines, they're experts at pulling the wool over people's eyes.'

'True, but I don't think so. I've met enough in my time to know when it's being faked. He's either telling us the truth or he's another level entirely. And right now I don't know which is scarier.'

Dexter sighed and nodded. 'You're right about the emails. It's weird that Martin would delete that one and not the others.'

'We'll know soon enough. Not that it'll explain anything either way.'

As if on cue, Dexter's phone rang. He answered it, looking at Caroline and nodding as he listened to the caller.

'That was them,' he said a few moments later. 'Gavin did send the email. It's still in his sent items.'

'So Martin deleted it?'

'It seems so,' Dexter replied. 'Like you say, it doesn't explain why.'

'No. No, it doesn't. Why would he want to remove all trace of that email, but not the others?'

'Maybe he was angry or annoyed and deleted it because Gavin called him a coward.'

'Do you think he'd be that bothered? It doesn't quite ring true.'

'Might've even been accidental.'

Caroline nodded slowly. It was a possibility, but she didn't think it likely. There was something there — something that didn't quite make sense — but it was just beyond her grasp.

41

For all Caroline's cautious confidence that they'd be able to ruffle Gavin Tanner's feathers, it hadn't worked. Even more disappointingly, their desperate search for evidence that might prove his guilt had been fruitless. In any case, they still had most of the day left before his twenty-four-hour custody clock ran out, and that was without seeking an extension.

Caroline's minimum target at this point was to secure enough evidence — even if only circumstantial — to secure an extra few hours on the clock. That way, they'd maximise their chances of finally nailing him. If all else failed and they had to bail him, they at least had his interview under caution, which could be used at a later date once evidence came to light. Some cases were slow to charge at the best of times, but dealing with fifteen-year-old evidence made that task all the more arduous. Still, she'd remain hopeful and quietly confident that they were on the right track.

A little later that morning, Caroline went to the toilet, where she found Sara Henshaw leaning against the cold tiled wall.

'Everything okay?' she asked.

'One of those days,' Sara replied. 'I just needed a few minutes. Hope that's alright.'

'Course. Are you okay? I don't want to sound rude, but you look like shit.' Sara had always been the calm, level-head of the team, a stable presence even when emotions ran high. To see her looking so brow-beaten was a shock to Caroline.

Sara smiled through one corner of her mouth. 'Thanks. I think.'

'Has something happened?'

Sara sighed. 'Sort of. I mean, yes. But not something that should've affected me, really.'

'Would it help to talk about it?' Caroline asked, standing beside her and leaning back against the wall, mirroring her stance.

'I dunno. Probably. But it's not something I ever do talk about, really. I had a call first thing this morning to say my mum had died.'

'Oh god, I'm so sorry.'

'No, it's okay. Not my real mum. I mean, yes, my real mum, but not my proper mum. I was adopted as a baby. My birth parents were drug addicts. Criminals. My birth dad died when I was a kid, but she hung on and caused as much havoc as she could for a few more years. Mum and Dad — the real ones, the ones who brought me up — called me this morning and told me she'd been found dead yesterday evening.'

'Christ. I don't know how you'd even go about processing something like that.'

Sara shrugged, her top rasping on the grouting of the tiled wall. 'I dunno. I don't even know how I feel, to be honest. There's sadness, I guess. It's always sad when a life ends like that, especially when it's been wasted. But at the same time it's the end of a chapter. I always knew who they were, but they never wanted to bother with me. They didn't care. As far as they were concerned, I was an unfortunate accident. But there was always that worry, that fear she might want to get back in touch and that I'd have to get to know her. I already knew enough to know that wouldn't be a good idea. But every time the phone rang, every time someone knocked on the door, there was always that fear at the back of my mind it might've been her. It'll take some getting used to realising it won't be.'

'Is that a good thing, then?' Caroline asked.

'I guess it is. It's sad I'll never know her. But then I never did know her, did I? And I never really wanted to, after the things I'd been told. But I guess that question'll never be answered now, will it?'

'No, I suppose not.'

'My parents were great. My real ones, I mean. Not my birth ones. They brought me up brilliantly, but it's amazing the things that still linger. So much that happens in those first few weeks and months goes on to shape your life for years. Decades. It's quite worrying, really.'

'What sort of things?' Caroline asked.

'Oh, I dunno really,' Sara replied, through a deep exhalation of breath. 'I don't do well at getting close to people, I guess. I don't trust easily. Maybe there's a fear of rejection in there somewhere.'

'I tell you what,' Caroline said, stepping away from the wall. 'How about we pop out for some fresh air for half an hour. Grab a coffee.'

Sara thought for a moment, then looked at her. 'I'd like that.'

A few minutes later, they were sitting in The Daily Grind, a short walk from the police station, towards the town centre. They'd found a quiet corner, and sat down with their drinks.

'Sometimes a change of scenery can help refresh the mind,' Caroline said. 'I mean, anything's better than staring at a toilet cubicle in the police bogs.'

'Oh, there are definitely some places round here that aren't,' Sara replied, smiling.

'How are your parents? I imagine it must be pretty weird for them hearing that news, not to mention having to pass it on to you.'

'Yeah. They're okay, I think. Like you say, weird situation. I got the sense they were relieved, in a way, but that their main concern was for me. It always has been.'

'They sound like good people,' Caroline said.

Sara smiled. 'They are. I've been very lucky. Just got to take that next step now, I guess. Not easy in this line of work, but hey.'

'You mean a partner?'

Sara nodded. 'Yeah. I know they always say coppers' relationships fall apart. The job owns you. Things like that. Sometimes I can see how true that is. But then again, other times I wonder how much the job has already taken over and stopped me from finding someone. It's not like I get much spare time.'

'I hope this isn't you telling me you're thinking of leaving.'

'Oh no. No, don't worry. Nothing like that. I just mean… Well, it's what I've always done. It's what I've always known. Seeking a sense of order and justice, maybe. Helping people and trying to give them the second chance I was given. I dunno. Between you and me, I've never really had a boyfriend. Not a proper one, anyway. Sometimes I look forward a few years and wonder how long I've got left before it's too late.'

'I dunno,' Caroline replied. 'I don't think it's ever too late.'

'It is for some things.'

'Kids?'

'Well, yeah.'

Caroline tried to rein in her thoughts. Concentrating on her own stresses in that area wouldn't help Sara in the slightest. Besides which, she already had two wonderful kids — the only two she'd ever wanted, she told herself. 'I'm sure it won't take you long to find someone. There are websites and apps and all sorts these days. You don't need to spend half as long at work as you do, either. You put far more in than you need to. I mean, maybe wait until we've charged on Operation Cruickshank, though.'

Sara laughed. 'Don't worry. I won't start knocking off early just yet.'

'I wouldn't blame you. You've earned it.'

'Besides, I still wonder whether the best option might be right under my nose.'

'Aidan?'

Sara nodded. 'Yeah. The more I think about it, the more it makes sense.'

Caroline bit her lip and tried to find the right words. She couldn't break the girl's heart by telling her Aidan was gay. But, then again, wasn't it worse to keep stringing her along with false hope? 'I… I'm really not sure he's interested in that way,' she said, finally.

'Oh. Oh. Okay. Has he said something to you?'

Caroline sighed. 'Sort of. I brought the subject up with him. Maybe it'll just take him time. I don't know. But I don't think it'll happen. Sorry.'

Sara looked at her. 'He's gay, isn't he?'

'Why do you say that?'

'I've had my suspicions for a while. A sixth sense, maybe. And I can see the way you're floundering about now, trying not to tell me.'

'Well, I…'

Caroline was saved by the ringing of her phone. She took it out of her pocket and looked at the screen. It was Dexter.

'Dex. What's up?'

'Guv, we've had a breakthrough on the Russell Speakman thing. You were right. He didn't fall down the stairs alone. We've just had a confession.'

42

Caroline stepped into the incident room with renewed energy and enthusiasm, Sara Henshaw trailing a few steps behind her.

'Dex,' she said, trying to catch her failing breath.

'You okay?' Dexter asked.

'Fine. Come on. Tell me.'

'Come here, sit down,' he said, giving her his seat. 'Okay. We had a woman come in at the front desk while you were out. Name of Ruby Clifford. She says she was there when Russell Speakman died. Said she's been racked with guilt for years, but managed to hide it. But she saw some stuff in one of the local Facebook groups about Martin's death and Amie being arrested.'

'Are you serious? We didn't release her name.'

'I know. It'll be the usual routine — nosy neighbour sees her being bundled into a police car, someone mentions it in passing to the local busybody, next thing you know there's some idiot gobbing off on social media thinking they're Roger Cook. Either way, it descended into the usual pile of dung, and someone mentioned she'd been linked with Russell Speakman's death a few years earlier.'

'Who the hell would do that?'

Dexter shrugged. 'We haven't looked into the details yet.'

'We'll need to. That stuff needs to be removed. I know they think they're being helpful, but if a defence brief gets wind of it, that's everything finished.'

'I know. We're on it.'

Caroline felt an unnatural rage boiling inside her. 'Do these people not realise their inability to keep their gobs shut can literally cause murderers to walk free?'

'I don't think they care about anything other than scoring internet points. But don't worry. We'll sort it. Either way, there might be a diamond buried in that steaming dog turd. Ruby Clifford says what she read brought it up to the surface and she wants to tell all.'

'Christ. Did she seem authentic?'

'Very. But she wants to deal directly with you.'

Caroline nodded, her breathing starting to return to normal. 'Okay. She still here?'

'Waiting in our finest suite as we speak.'

'Alright. Bring her through to an interview room.'

Having taken a few minutes to regain herself, Caroline made her way down to the interview room with Dexter. As they opened the door and stepped inside, they got their first look at Ruby Clifford. To Caroline, she seemed like a woman who was nervous, but looking forward to getting a huge weight off her shoulders.

'Hi, Ruby. I'm Detective Inspector Caroline Hills. This is my colleague, Detective Sergeant Dexter Antoine. We understand you wanted to speak to us with regards to the investigation into the death of Russell Speakman, is that right?'

Ruby dug her fingernails into the back of her hand. 'Yes. Christ, I don't even know where to begin. I was a girlfriend of Russell's. One of many. I... I was round at his that evening. We had an argument, because I'd found out he'd been cheating on me. My friend, Layla, had seen him kissing another girl in town. It... God, it sounds so bad saying it like this. It was Amie Murray who she saw him with, so when I heard the police had been on to her and brought her in, I thought, Good. Let her have it. I thought she deserved to suffer for what she'd done. Obviously now I know that's not really a rational thing to think, but by the time things had died down there was no way I could just call the police and admit what happened. And then the more time that passes... it just becomes impossible.'

'Okay. Can you talk us through what happened?' Caroline asked.

'I can try. There are bits I remember like it was yesterday, but other things are just blank.'

'Do your best.'

Ruby thought for a moment, and seemed to be

composing herself. Caroline watched her adam's apple bob as she swallowed, then spoke. As she did, she stared at the floor in the corner of the room, visions and memories playing in her mind.

'He invited me over. Fairly last minute. I think he'd probably had an argument with another girl of his and I was the only one who was free. I wanted to bring it up with him — what my friend had seen — but I didn't know what to say. And eventually I told him. I told him what Layla saw. He said I was crazy. He'd gone upstairs. He always tried running away from problems. Never wanted to face up to them. I told him to look me in the eye and tell me it wasn't true, but he couldn't. His phone was charging in his bedroom, and I knew there'd be texts on it from his other girls. He was always so secretive with it. So I went to go into his room and get it, to prove what he'd been up to, and he grabbed me. I thought... I don't know what I thought. I've played this moment over in my head so many times over the years. So many times. Maybe I thought he was going to hit me. Maybe I wanted to... I don't know. But I swung my arm round and hit him. I don't know if it was just the angle, or where it caught him, or what, but he lost his balance. He was at the top of the stairs and he lost his balance. It all seemed to happen so slowly, but I couldn't do anything about it. I can still hear the sound of him falling. By the time I realised what was happening it was too late. I could tell, just by looking at him. You can sort of tell, can't you? When someone's dead. You can tell.'

The silence in the room was heavy. Caroline and Dexter could feel the weight of the secret Ruby had been carrying with her for fifteen years. It wouldn't do anyone any good to tell her Russell had still been alive at that point.

'Ruby. I know this is a difficult question, and one that's probably impossible to answer, but do you think hitting Russell knocked him down the stairs?'

Ruby shook her head slightly. 'I don't think so. I don't know. I wasn't facing him. But I didn't think it was that hard. I think he tried to swerve it, but went too far and slipped. I didn't even mean to hit him. Not really. It was just an instinctive reaction. I thought he was going to hurt me. I keep telling myself that. That it was self-defence. An accident. I believe that. I really do. It keeps it at bay, too, for a bit. Sometimes it flares up again and I panic. I melt down. And now, when I heard you were looking into what happened again, it got too much. I had to say something. I needed the truth to be out there.'

Caroline looked at Dexter, and they exchanged a knowing glance. Would there be any benefit in charging Ruby with anything? What good would it do? She certainly wasn't a cold-blooded murderer. She probably hadn't even killed Russell Speakman. Not directly. Although Caroline had always valued justice over everything else, she had to question whether that would be just in any sense of the word.

But it did help. They now knew what had happened to Russell Speakman. And they knew for certain that the

Tanners hadn't had any involvement. In Caroline's eyes, that drastically lowered their chances of having been involved in the murder of Martin Forbes, too. It was all a highly unfortunate set of coincidences. But that didn't leave them any closer to finding their killer. Far from it.

43

After interviewing Ruby, Dexter and Caroline stepped outside into the car park for some much-needed fresh air.

'Not hard to see she was telling the truth there,' Dexter said. 'You could see how difficult it was for her.'

'I know,' Caroline replied. 'Problem is it opens up a whole can of worms now. By rights, that should go through CPS and the courts. It'd be overturning the coroner's verdict.'

'That said accidental death, didn't it? I don't see how this was anything other than accidental. Slightly different circumstances, but same outcome. In any case, it's up to us to pass it on to the CPS if we think a charge is necessary. If we're comfortable no crime was committed... Well.'

'No, I agree. She needed to get it off her chest. That's the main thing. My biggest worry now is that it throws Operation Cruickshank into disarray,' Caroline said, bracing herself against the cold, which was quickly starting to set in. 'If Amie Tanner wasn't involved in the death of Russell Speakman, it makes it far less likely she or Gavin were involved here, too. It was the "far too much of a coincidence" thing that was driving that. Now we don't even have the coincidence. All we have is a brief argument between Amie and Martin at work a few days earlier. And who hasn't had a barney at work before?'

'We still can't discount Gavin. Sure, it might not be linked with Speakman, but we've got him at the scene. Means, motive, opportunity — he's got the lot. And there's always the possibility Ruby's been set up to confess.'

'I'm not so sure,' Caroline replied. 'We know Gavin was at the scene where Martin's body was found, but we're also pretty certain he was killed elsewhere. What if he's been set up?'

'Set up by who?' Dexter asked. 'Gavin admitted to sending the emails to Martin and arranging to meet him. He told us that much.'

'Exactly. Why would he make it so obvious and traceable? Even the forensics don't add up. The mud on his car tyres is a match to the viaduct, but there's nothing on his shoes.'

'He said he didn't get out of the car, though.'

'If he killed Martin, he'd have to.'

'Maybe he cleaned his shoes.'

'On a forensically pure scale? Come off it. Why would he go to that effort to sterilise his shoes but leave his car tyres? Something doesn't sit right here, Dex. Call it a hunch if you like, but there's something else to this.'

'I'm looking forward to you telling all this to Arnold.'

'Don't, Dex. Just don't. The thought's already crossed my mind more than once. How much time have we lost on this now? Christ's sake. I can hear him now, banging on about my "condition" and how we need to work as a team, use wider resources, stop chasing hunches. He'll have me back on medical leave.'

'Nah, he won't,' Dexter said, trying to placate her. 'Don't worry about it. We've got your back. You'll be good.'

Caroline looked at him and smiled. 'Thanks, Dex. But seriously, don't. It's not worth blotting your own copy book over.'

Before Dexter could reply, the door opened and Aidan came out into the car park.

'Guv, we've just had a call from Amie Tanner's mum. She says Amie's gone missing.'

44

Back in the warmth of the incident room, Aidan relayed what had come in through a 999 emergency call.

'Okay, so the details as we understand them are that Amie's mum has been at the house helping out with the kids while Gavin's having a well-earned rest in our luxury holiday suite downstairs. She says Amie left home at her usual time this morning to go to work. Nothing out of the ordinary at all. At ten o'clock she's not arrived at work, so work call her mobile and get no response. Lunchtime, they call her home landline and the mum picks up. Says she left for work at the usual time. So now mum's panicking. She calls her mobile, which work have already tried, but it's off. She said she didn't want to cause a panic or waste police time, but the more she thought about it the more concerning it was, so eventually she picks up the phone and calls the police.'

'Alright,' Caroline said. 'Speak to the network. Get cell tracking on Amie's phone. Let's find out where it went off grid. You're ANPR trained, aren't you?'

'I am. I'll run her reg number and see what comes back.'

'Good work. Thanks, Aidan. If we can track down where she went missing, we can start to look at why. No accidents reported on the roads, I presume?'

'Not that I've heard of. Nothing called in, anyway.'

'Alright. That increases the chances that this was deliberate, either on her part or someone else's. She can't have gone far. She had to surrender her passport when she was bailed.'

'Good point,' Aidan replied.

'So the two most likely outcomes here are that Amie has decided to go on the run, which would be odd seeing as we'd all but discounted her as a suspect, or that she's been taken. That's a whole lot more concerning, especially as she either *is* our killer, or the killer's still out there. Sara, let's have another look at the known relationships chart. Work on the assumption that whoever killed Martin Forbes has also taken Amie. Who'd want to harm them both? What are the connections? Let's start from that point and see where it takes us.'

Sara nodded. 'Alright.'

Aidan stood up and came back over. 'Guv, there's a hit from vehicle mounted ANPR about an hour ago. It picked it up on the A6003 at Preston. Looks like it's parked up in a lay-by.'

'Brilliant, Aidan. Thanks. Dex, get your coat back on. We're going for a drive.'

45

Shortly after they'd arrived in the village of Preston, just a few miles south of Oakham on the road to Uppingham, Caroline saw the lay-by. It was right outside a row of houses, and presumably intended for the owners' parking, but she immediately recognised Amie Tanner's car. She pulled in behind it and switched off her engine.

'No-one in it,' Dexter said.

'Good. Last thing I want today is to find another body.'

'Maybe she's visiting a friend. Does she have any connections with anyone here?'

'I don't know,' Caroline replied, stepping out of her car and walking over to look at Amie's, being careful not to touch it. 'Call uniform down here, Dex. We're going to need to do a door-to-door. See if any of the neighbours here saw anything. Someone must've done.'

As Dexter called in Caroline's request, an elderly man stepped out of one of the houses and walked over to them.

'You police?' he called.

'Yes, do you live here?' Caroline asked.

'I do. You got a badge?'

Caroline showed him her ID card.

'Alright. Good,' the man said. 'I figured you was either police or criminals, the way you're looking round the car.'

Caroline noticed he'd given a particular look in Dexter's direction, and sincerely hoped it wasn't connected with his race. 'Did you see who parked it here?' she asked him, keen to get to the point.

'Happen I did, aye. A woman. Attractive, like. Pretty young thing.'

'What time was this?' Dexter asked.

'Oooh, I reckon not long before nine. Quarter to, perhaps. Seemed odd, because most of the cars leave not long before that. Off to work, see. Bit strange to see someone arriving at that time.'

'And did you notice what she looked like?'

'Aye. Blonde hair. Extraordinary buttocks.'

As much as she found the man's description distasteful, Caroline had to admit it did at least confirm it was Amie Tanner he'd seen.

'Did you see where she went?'

'Aye. Off with her friend.'

Caroline and Dexter exchanged a look. 'Friend?'

'The bloke in the other car. They both pulled in together, got out and looked at her car just like you was there, stood around for a minute or so, then she got into his car and off they went.'

'Did she seem to go willingly or was there a struggle at all?'

'Seemed alright to me,' the man replied. 'He didn't have to bundle her in or anything, if that's what you mean.'

'What sort of car did they get into?'

'Blimey, all these questions. She a wrong'un or something?'

Caroline could feel herself losing patience quickly. 'Please just answer the questions. What sort of car was it?'

The man shrugged. 'Dunno. I dunno cars, me. It were blue, I can tell you that. Estate, I think. You can always tell them from the side.'

'And the man? Did you get a look at him?'

'Not with these eyes,' the man replied. 'Sorry. Wasn't really paying much attention to him, if you know what I mean.'

'Okay. Thanks. Which way did you say they went?'

The man pointed down the road. 'Down that way,' he said. 'Towards Uppingham. Maybe have a look down there.'

46

Caroline and Dexter got back into her car, glad for the warmth. They'd put out a call for local units to keep eyes open for a blue estate car, as well as sightings of Amie Tanner. Although their instinct might've been to head straight off in the direction of Uppingham, it had been quite some time since Amie and her abductor had left, and they could've been absolutely anywhere by now.

Officers were already on their way to the scene, where they'd be able to search the car properly and take an official statement from the man they'd spoken to, who'd eventually identified himself as Eric Darnforth.

'It's got to be someone she knows,' Dexter said. 'She's not the sort of woman who'd get into a stranger's car on a whim. She'd sooner beat him black and blue.'

'I've got to agree it narrows the field somewhat,' Caroline replied. 'Hang on.'

Caroline got out of the car and walked back over to

Amie's. She peered through the windows, careful not to touch anything. Then she crouched down onto the floor and looked under the car before getting up and knocking on Eric Darnforth's door.

'Sorry to bother you again,' she said as he answered, 'but I don't suppose you saw either of them using a mobile phone, did you?'

'Don't happen I did, no, love. Why's that?'

'Just wondered. Did either of them put anything anywhere? Throw something into bushes, perhaps? Anything else suspicious?'

'No, not that I noticed. Like I say, they parked up, right where you are now. She got out of her car, he got out of his. They looked round hers for a bit, then got into his, sat for a minute or so then drove off.'

'Did you see what they were doing for that minute before they drove off?'

Eric almost laughed. 'No, no chance. Like I say, these eyes aren't what they used to be. Plus the light's too low that time of morning. Get all that glare off the glass, you know.'

Caroline forced a smile, said her goodbyes then headed back to her car. If nothing else, it would be a fun hour or two for whoever got to take that statement.

47

Caroline's head was a mess. Focus was impossible. She didn't know how much of it was down to the case itself and how much was caused by her recovery and her present mental state, but it wasn't entirely out of the ordinary for her at the best of times. It was almost the opposite of the calm before the storm: it was the fog and confusion that came before the moment of clarity which would unlock everything else. And she felt she was getting close to that point.

'We're halfway there anyway,' she said as she pulled back out onto the road and headed towards Uppingham.

'They'll be long gone by now. They were probably heading for the A47.'

'Probably. But I don't think it's them I'm looking for.'

Dexter looked across at her. 'Are you okay?'

'I'm fine. There's just... Just something I need to check.'

A few minutes later, they pulled up outside the offices of Allure Design. They were met by Monique, who quickly hid her initial awkwardness and embarrassment with an over-the-top show of enthusiasm.

'How wonderful to see you again,' Monique said, welcoming them with a little too much energy. 'How can I be of assistance?'

'We just wanted to ask you a few more questions, if we may. I hope it's not too inconvenient.'

'No, of course. *Audentes fortuna iuvat.*'

'Sorry?'

'Fortune favours the bold.'

'Alright, Doris. I'll be honest, I've never really understood that one in English, never mind a language that doesn't exist anymore.' Caroline watched as Monique shrunk like a snowball in the Sahara. 'Quick question. Is your IT chap in today? Tom Mackintosh.'

'He's not, I'm afraid. I can ask him to give you a call when he's back in, though?'

Caroline smiled. 'That's fine. Don't worry. He has quite a few days off, doesn't he?'

'Perks of the job, I guess. He's been here a long time and things seem to work just fine. Plus he can do his job from anywhere, really. He just goes in through his VPN thingie and he's away. He did explain it to me once, but it went well over my head.'

'And mine, too,' Caroline replied. 'How long's he been working here?'

'Oh, easily ten years. If not more. Yes, he started a few months before me, so it must be nearly twelve years now.'

'Is that fairly normal here? Do staff tend to stick around?'

'Oh yes. We don't have a high turnover in that respect. I think Amie's probably one of our newest staff members, and she's been here years. It was Tom who got her the job, actually.'

Caroline started to feel the cogs turn. 'Really? Did they know each other before?'

'Yes, from school I think. It's a while ago, but I seem to recall he recommended her to Martin.'

'I see. Is that normal?'

Monique shrugged. 'What's normal? And in any case it seems to have worked out well. *Creo quia absurdum est.* I think that sums this place up.'

'I'll have to take your word for it,' Caroline said, trying her hardest not to look in the direction of Dexter, who was doing his best not to laugh.

'It means "I believe because it is absurd". It's effectively the opposite of Occam's razor. It's not always the simplest or most logical solution that turns out to be right.'

The sudden hit of clarity was both invigorating and alarming. 'Monique, do you know where Tom is today?'

'At home, I presume. He called in to say he wouldn't be in the office. He's a bit unpredictable like that, but he always does us the courtesy of letting us know, even if it is a little bit last minute.'

'How last minute?'

'Last night, after he'd already got home.'

Caroline shot a look at Dexter, who seemed a little slower to cotton on, but had noticed Caroline was on to something. 'And is that normal for him?' she asked Monique.

'Oh yes. That holiday he had in Scotland the other week? He decided to let us know the night before. I mean, he can do his work from anywhere, really, but still.'

Caroline felt her heart hammering in her chest. All of a sudden, things were starting to make sense.

48

Caroline closed the door of her car and held her hand in the air. She needed to think and she didn't want Dexter interrupting her train of thought unnecessarily. But it was the ringing of her phone that jolted her back to the here and now. She looked at the screen. It was Aidan.

'Aidan. What is it?' she said, immediately realising she'd perhaps sounded a little brusque.

'We've had data back from one of the online nurseries we contacted about those roses, the Black Baccaras? There's a small handful of people within a reasonable radius of Rutland, but only one who's ordered repeatedly over the past few years, just before Valentine's Day.'

'Let me guess,' Caroline said, rubbing her temples with her free hand. 'Tom Mackintosh.'

'Well, it says Thomas here, but yeah,' Aidan replied, sounding slightly deflated.

'He's the IT guy from Allure Design.'

'Why would he have been sending roses to Amie Tanner every year since her dad died?'

Caroline sighed. 'I don't know. Presumably for the same reason he got her the job at Allure in the first place. And the reason why the email from Gavin Tanner to Martin Forbes saying he hadn't turned up had been deleted at Martin's end, but not Gavin's. Because Tom had access to Martin's computers and accounts.'

'Christ. Where are you? Did you find the car?'

'Yeah. We're in Uppingham. Tom didn't turn up for work today. He called in at about nine o'clock and said he'd be working from home, but there's no way that's where he is. It's him who's taken Amie. I know it is. Think about it. She willingly got into someone's car, so it must've been someone she knew. I bet you any money he's made damn sure he was driving behind her and has flashed her over and told her he's spotted something wrong with her car. "Jump in with me, we're going the same way anyway". I can see it now. Aidan, can we get an emergency trace on Tom's phone please?'

'Alright. I'll go to the Chief Super now.'

'Cheers. Please be as quick as you can.'

They sat in silence for a minute or two, listening to the sound of the occasional passing car.

'Want to place a bet?' Caroline said.

Dexter shrugged. 'Wouldn't like to guess. I doubt he'll have gone into Uppingham. Not if he wanted to get away and take her somewhere. We know he's not taken her to work, so it'd be too risky going that way. If he took the

A47, he's heading towards either Leicester or Peterborough. I don't think he'll be going to either city, but there're a thousand places along that corridor where he could've turned off. Thing is, the second he doesn't go straight over that Uppingham roundabout, Amie's spooked. As far as she knows, her colleague's giving her a lift to work.'

'Shortcut? Petrol en route?'

'More like a longcut. And the petrol station's in the centre of Uppingham. They'd literally drive straight past it on the normal route in. My money's on the A47. The only question then is how he managed to get away with it. He's either come up with a cracking excuse, threatened her or incapacitated her.'

'Last one's difficult while driving,' Caroline replied, leaving them both to think for a few moments longer. 'I just feel like we should be doing something other than sitting here,' she said eventually.

'Got to sit tight. Can't risk flying off in the wrong direction. Phone trace won't take long.'

Moments later, Dexter's phone rang. It was a response from the control room. He listened and jotted down a couple of details, then ended the call.

'Right. Tom's phone's been off since six this morning. Last place it was online was at his home. Amie's, on the other hand, was on until a few minutes before nine. It goes off on the A47, east of the Uppingham roundabout.'

'Okay,' Caroline said, piecing the puzzle together in her mind. 'South from Preston to the Uppingham roundabout, left onto the A47 heading east. Peterborough direction. Train station? Unlikely. CCTV, too many people. Too much of a risk of his car being spotted. His phone's been off for hours, so he's keen not to be seen or found. He's planned this. He'll be going far away from it all.' She pulled her phone out of her pocket and opened Google Maps. She ran her finger along the A47 corridor, looking for possible places Tom might have gone. Her heart jumped in her chest as she saw the green area just south of the junction with the A43. 'Fineshade Wood. Where do I know that name, Dex?'

'Isn't that the place he was talking about when we first met him? I thought he said he camps out there sometimes. Yeah. Yeah, he did. He said you should get one of those Swedish huts.'

'Danish shelters.'

'Same thing.'

'We can't go in heavy. What if he's armed?'

Dexter's eyes narrowed. 'Tom Mackintosh? What's he armed with, a floppy disk?'

Caroline started the car. 'He's a keen survivalist. He'll have hunting knives. We're going to need armed response.'

As Caroline pulled out onto the road, Dexter nodded and made the call.

49

As Caroline drove, Dexter had put the call out for extra officers to attend the scene. Although it was just over the border in Northamptonshire, county boundaries were largely irrelevant, especially when the crime had been committed within their jurisdiction of Rutland.

With Fineshade Wood covering well over one thousand acres, it would be almost impossible to find Tom and Amie without a huge number of reinforcements. With Tom's mindset and intentions still unknown, they couldn't risk spooking him and potentially endangering Amie.

A little over ten minutes later, they arrived at the entrance road to Fineshade Wood, a narrow, single-track road with passing places scattered along the length of it — not that Caroline had any intention of letting anyone pass. The sun would soon be starting to set, and as they crossed over the River Welland, she wondered if this was the route Tom and Amie had taken, wondered if she'd been right.

She knew in her gut she was, but her gut had been wrong before.

They reached the Forestry Commission's *Welcome* sign and forked left, towards the main car park.

'I think the shelters are over that way,' Dexter said, pointing to their left. He'd brought up a map of Fineshade on his phone.

'Okay. We can't go muscling in,' Caroline replied. 'We need to know if he's been here first. Where's the reception?'

Dexter looked at her, trying to work out if she was serious. It quickly became clear she was. 'Reception? For the woods?'

'Well I don't know how these things work, do I? There must be something somewhere. We need to speak to someone.'

'There's a building over there where we came in,' Dexter said. 'Think the sign says *café*. But I doubt they'll be sitting in there sipping a couple of chai lattes and talking about last night's Eastenders. You okay?' he asked as Caroline bit into the skin at the side of her fingernail.

'I'm fine. How long til the cavalry arrives?'

'No idea. Didn't say.'

'It'll be getting dark soon. We can't go flashing torches around in the woods. He'll spot us a mile off.'

'What do you suggest?' Dexter asked, the light levels starting to drop, and another bitter night beginning to set in.

Caroline thought for a moment. She knew what was

expected. She knew what the rulebook said. But she also knew what was right in this situation.

'He knows us,' she said, finally. 'We've met. We've spoken. Surely we've got a better chance at talking him round than armed response have wading in with guns.'

Dexter made a non-committal murmur. 'It's a huge risk. We're potentially putting ourselves and Amie in danger.'

'I dunno, Dex. I think going in mob-handed is riskier here. He doesn't want to hurt Amie. It doesn't sit right. The roses on Valentine's Day, getting her a job, killing Martin Forbes and trying to frame her husband. He's been wooing her in his own weird way for years. He wants to be with her.'

Dexter narrowed his eyes. 'What, in a freezing cold hut?'

'Danish shelter. And yes. He can't exactly take her back to his place, can he? That's the first place we'd look.'

'Yeah, because he knows the net's closing in and we're onto him. If he's getting desperate, he could do anything.'

'Exactly,' Caroline said, staring through the windscreen towards the trees. 'And that's why we need to act now.'

50

'This is ridiculous. I can't see a bloody thing,' Caroline said a short while later, as she and Dexter stepped off the footpath and started to walk towards the area of the woods that housed the Danish shelters.

'Permission to say I told you so?' Dexter replied.

'Absolutely not.'

'It shouldn't be too much further. We should probably start to keep our voices down. There we are, look. Can you see the campfire?'

Caroline cursed as she stumbled slightly, almost twisting her ankle. 'Would he really take her somewhere like this, Dex? From the way he was talking, I presumed it was right in the middle of nowhere. We're barely a few yards from the main path here.'

'Easy in, easy out. Plus he knows the area like the back of his hand. He could head out deeper if he needed to, but why wouldn't you take advantage of a hut when the weather's like this? And don't say it. I know what they're called.'

Caroline let go of a breath she didn't realise she'd been holding. Her whole body was tense, and the cold wasn't helping any. She stretched her arms out straight, feeling the tightness ease on the insides of her elbows. 'It's almost hiding in plain sight,' she said. 'I think we can safely assume he hasn't drugged her or knocked her out. There'd be no way he could drag her over there, or that someone wouldn't see her and report it.'

'That means he's almost certainly threatened her with a weapon of some sort,' Dexter replied. 'You sure it was a good idea to call off armed response?'

Caroline thought for a moment, more as a matter of courtesy than anything else. She knew the risks. She knew it went against conventional protocol. But she also felt she knew how Tom Mackintosh operated. It had all started to make a lot of sense. If it went wrong, Derek Arnold would have her strung up. He'd been strangely loyal and willing to put his neck on the line for her up until now, but even he would have his limits. There was no way she'd be able to get away with making a reckless mistake that cost Tom or Amie their lives.

Tom had thought many things through carefully. He'd clearly been infatuated with Amie for years. But he'd also been impulsive. He'd leapt on Gavin's request to meet Martin Forbes and used it to frame him for murder. And it had worked, for a time. He'd acted quickly to kidnap Amie when the net started closing in. Caroline felt she knew his mind, and it was clear to her that it needed calming. No rash moves, no gangs of police officers, no weapons.

'Yeah, I'm sure,' she said. 'Let's go in.'

51

As they neared the clearing, they took in the scene in front of them. A large campfire roared in the middle of the clearing, with a series of wooden structures surrounding it. Each was almost completely enclosed, but open on the side closest to the fire, like a huge wooden trough turned on its side. Caroline could see how these could be cosy, given the right conditions.

She'd been about to turn to Dexter and tell him she didn't think anyone was there, when she noticed movement. It was the unmistakeable gangly figure of Tom, the bright orange glow of the fire flickering across his face as he stoked it.

Before she could convince herself otherwise, she stepped forward and into the clearing.

It took a moment before Tom spotted her, but his reaction didn't surprise her. It was as she thought: a young man who'd always wanted, always tried, to do the right thing but who'd got in well over his neck.

'It's okay, Tom,' she said. 'We just wanted to check you and Amie are okay.'

'How did you find us?' Tom replied, his voice hesitant, slightly shaky.

'It's our job. Amie's family reported her missing. They're worried about her.'

Tom shifted his weight to the other foot. 'She's fine,' he said. 'She's a lot safer with me than she is with them, that's for sure.' There was a hint of venom in his reply which made Caroline uneasy. The light was difficult at best, and she didn't know if it was because she was expecting something, but she felt sure he had something in his hand. Some sort of weapon, perhaps. Either way, she couldn't take any chances.

'Does she think that too?' she asked him.

'She doesn't know what's best for her. Not yet. But she will do.'

'Are you sure? It's bitter out here, Tom. She could be frightened. Scared. She's got a family who are worried for her. Why don't we do what's best for her, eh?'

Tom's eyes narrowed. 'You don't know what's best for her. No-one does.'

'How about you let me see her and ask her, then? I just want to make sure she's okay,' Caroline replied, her heart beating heavily in her chest. She hoped her nerves weren't showing. She needed to maintain control of the situation. Tom looked at her, and she could almost see the cogs turning in his mind as he tried to suss out her intentions. 'We just want to make sure she's safe.'

Tom raised his arms slightly, and Caroline got her first sure glimpse of what was in his hand. It was almost certainly a camping knife. 'Alright,' he said, far more casually than she'd expected. 'Come and have a look.'

'Will you put the knife down first, please, Tom?'

'Nope.'

'I really think it'd be safer,' Caroline replied.

'I don't.'

Caroline turned her head towards Dexter, who gave her the slightest, almost imperceptible nod. *I've got your back* were the unspoken words. She stepped forward and watched as Tom turned slightly, opening his body towards one of the shelters. As she got closer, she began to make out Amie's form inside it, the flickering campfire light occasionally giving her better glimpses. She saw the light playing on Amie's eyes, looking back at her. They were wide, watery. Scared.

As Caroline stepped closer, she could see Amie's mouth had been bound with tape, her hands still underneath a woollen blanket. Caroline wouldn't have been surprised if they were tied together. She wanted to ask Amie if she was okay, but she could clearly see she wasn't. In any case, the last thing they needed was for her to become a live wire and send the situation spiralling out of control. Caroline needed to keep things calm and level. If they could get the knife from Tom, they'd be ahead. Right now, though, they were far from it.

'That'll do. No closer,' Tom said.

Caroline's heart sank. She'd been hoping Dexter might manage to somehow outflank Tom, but he was doing all-too-good a job of keeping everyone well within his sights. Now she was between Tom and Amie. On the face of it, she was in a position to protect her, but in reality she knew it was more akin to getting between a lion and its prey.

Amie was trying to mumble or murmur something, but it was inaudible beneath the tape that bound her mouth. She looked more angry than scared now, having seemingly grown in confidence since Caroline and Dexter had arrived, and Caroline suspected it might be best for the tape to stay on, lest Amie say the wrong thing and send the situation spiralling.

'What's this all about, Tom? What's the end game?' Caroline asked.

'I'm keeping her safe. Protected,' Tom replied.

'She doesn't look like she feels safe, Tom. She looks scared. Upset. Is that what you want?'

Tom looked towards his quarry, and Caroline noticed a poignant look cross his face. It was the first time she'd seen him contemplate something outside of his own head. It looked almost like empathy.

'She'll be fine. She doesn't know it now, but this is what's best for her.'

'She has a husband and kids, Tom. They miss her.'

Tom scoffed. 'He doesn't care about Amie. All he's ever wanted is a trophy wife. You should see how he behaves around them. She deserves better. So much better. She always has.'

Tom's voice was tinged with emotion, and Caroline thought she saw a way in. 'You've always loved her, haven't you?' she said, her voice soft and genuine.

Tom nodded a little, his eyes glistening. 'Always,' he croaked.

'It must be hard. I can't imagine how difficult it must be watching the person you love go through life without you.'

As she spoke, thoughts of Mark filled her head. She'd been pushing him away. She knew she had. But at the same time there had been nothing she could do to stop herself. She'd spent so long wrapped up in her own head, she'd failed to see the small, simple ways in which she could have made things better for both of them.

'You have no idea,' Tom said. 'No idea at all what it's been like.'

Caroline let out a small sigh. 'I think I've come closer than I've realised. If you love her, Tom, you need to do what's best for her. She's scared. She's upset. She wants to be at home.'

Tom shook his head vigorously, and spoke between desperate breaths. 'No. That's not best for her. I know what's best for her. I've known her longer than anyone.'

'Tom, can I ask you something?' Caroline asked calmly.

Tom nodded.

'Did you kill Martin Forbes and make it look like Gavin had done it?'

Tom looked at Amie, holding eye contact with her for a few moments. Caroline could almost see the burden weighing down on him as he began to try to explain.

'Martin wasn't a good man,' he said, shaking his head. There was almost a childish quality about the way he spoke. 'Nuh-uh. Most people saw one side of him, but some saw a different one. Women, mostly. Amie,' he said, looking at her. 'I saw the way he was towards her. I always notice the way people are towards her. She's my world. Always has been. He couldn't take it that she wasn't interested. He'd always had his way with women, but not with Amie. Amie's too strong. She's too good. She didn't give in. But it didn't make him stop. I saw the way he was towards her at work. He victimised her. Everything was her fault. He picked holes in every little thing, tried to make her life hell. All because she wouldn't sleep with him. Because she's good. She's a good girl. A good little girl.'

Caroline looked at Amie, whose face told a story that was anything but. She seemed to be growing ever more furious, buoyed with a new confidence now she and Dexter were here and fighting her corner. Caroline knew she had to keep Amie calm, too — possibly even calmer than Tom, as otherwise she was likely to provide the tinderbox that'd blow the whole situation apart.

The quietude of the woods was pierced by the shrill ringing of Caroline's mobile phone. Instinctively, she took it out of her coat pocket. It was Mark. Ringing to say dinner was on the table, no doubt, complaining that she was late home again without bothering to tell him.

'Don't answer that,' Tom replied. 'Who is it? Police?'

'No, it's my husband.'

'Don't answer.'

Caroline pressed the rocker switch on the side of her phone, switching it to vibrate-only mode.

'What about Russell Speakman, Tom?' she asked, trying to change the conversation slightly towards something she was sure she already knew the answer to, and which might help placate Amie somewhat.

Tom's eyes narrowed. 'What about him?'

'Did you kill him too?'

'No,' he replied, looking almost offended. 'No, of course I didn't. I knew that'd never last. Not with how many women he had on the go. I knew sooner or later she'd come to me. It was just a matter of waiting. It was sheer luck what happened to him. When I found out about the others, I told that gobby cow Layla I'd seen Russell and Amie kissing in town. I knew she was best friends with Ruby Clifford, and that she'd take the credit and say she saw it with her own eyes. I just wanted to make life hell for him. I didn't want him to die. I didn't kill him.'

'I know, Tom. Someone's already come forward and admitted to what happened. It was an accident.'

'Gavin?' Tom asked.

'No, not Gavin.'

'I never liked him,' he replied, lost in his thoughts once again. 'Horrible prick. Always doing the white knight act, there to save the day. He did bugger all. He just wanted his leggy blonde. He's corrupted her. He doesn't know the real Amie. He doesn't know her at all.'

'I know. But he's her husband, Tom.'

'He's nothing. He's worse than nothing. You know what? I didn't need to make it look like Gavin had killed Martin, because the stupid prick had set it up for himself.'

Caroline glanced at Amie, hoping she wasn't about to see an explosion. On the contrary, she appeared to have been stunned into submission.

Tom continued, oblivious. 'I knew what Martin was up to. I wanted to take him down. For the way he treated everyone. Women. The way he treated Amie. I'd thought of a few things, but nothing quite seemed to gel. I don't know if I ever would've gone through with any of it. Probably not. But then when I saw Gavin's email land in Martin's inbox, it all made sense.'

'You've been monitoring and accessing Martin's private emails?' Caroline asked.

'Obviously,' Tom replied, with a look that seemed surprised there'd be any other possibility. 'It made so much sense. I knew which route Martin took on his runs. I knew where he'd be going. I knew Gavin would be waiting at the viaduct. There'd be traces of him being there. The emails that showed he set it all up. It seemed too good to be true. I had the ultimate opportunity. The chance to get rid of them both.'

By now, Caroline could see Amie starting to get more and more agitated. She knew Tom's words were causing more harm than good right now, but the strength and detail of his confession was too powerful to deny him.

'I parked up in a lay-by on the Barrowden road, as you come straight out of Seaton. It's a narrow lane. No traffic. I saw Martin coming down the hill. Stupid little head torch bobbing about. As he got closer, I switched on my headlights, then got out of the car. He couldn't see because of the headlights, but I had a baseball bat in my hand. As he got closer, I swung it. He didn't have a chance. He hit the ground and started gurgling. Christ, it made a hell of a noise. A large part of me wanted to leave him there, at the side of the road. I was desperate to just get out of there. But I knew I couldn't. I knew this was only one small part of the plan, and I needed to stick to it. The last thing I wanted was him yelling or getting back up, so I wrapped my arm around his neck and squeezed. Just squeezed. I thought he'd try to fight back, but there was nothing. He didn't even lift his arms. He was gurgling but his whole body was limp. Then... then he just stopped.

'I'd lined the back of the car with plastic sheeting. It's an estate. Handy for camping. Took me ages to drag him round and put him in the back, but I managed it in the end. Didn't want anyone seeing him. I could tell he was going. His eyes were rolling around in his head and he was starting to turn blue. I just remember his fitness watch pinging, asking him if he'd stopped exercising because he was still and his heart rate had dropped. I actually found that funny. I don't know if that makes me a bad person. But I took it off him and switched it off. I don't know how much data those things store. I panicked it might reveal where he was when he died. I shut the boot, got back in and kept the engine on, just in case. If someone came along, I knew I'd need to get away quickly in case he made any noise. I knew he wouldn't, though. You know when someone isn't coming back. I waited a bit. I wanted to make sure Gavin would be gone.

'And that's when I worried I'd done the wrong thing. I knew I had to keep calm, though. I needed to. So I started driving. I pulled away really carefully, I remember that. The way you do when you've just packed the car full. Like you've got a delicate load. I turned left just before Seaton and headed back round towards the viaduct, where I knew Gavin had arranged to meet him. I could see his car there, so I carried on past and went round again, more slowly this time. As I came round towards Seaton the second time, I saw his car going over the crossroads, up towards Glaston and the A47. That's when I knew he was heading home. So I carried on round to the viaduct, and left Martin there. He looked peaceful. I know it sounds strange, but he did.

'Then I went home. I packed all the plastic sheeting into small cardboard boxes and lit a bonfire at the end of the garden. Plenty of wood, too. And the baseball bat. I knew the plastic would stink otherwise.'

Caroline nodded to herself. Of course. The odd smell of stale smoke she'd noticed when she met Tom hadn't been cannabis. It was the remnants of the previous night's bonfire, tinged with burnt plastic. The dirty bastard hadn't even washed or changed his clothes.

'Then you deleted the email,' she said, continuing the story for him.

Tom nodded. 'I knew the police would probably be after the computers and stuff. I'm not daft. I only ever accessed his stuff either while I was at work, or through the work VPN so it looked like it'd come from there. I saw the email Gavin sent, calling Martin a coward for not turning up. I knew that wouldn't look good, so I deleted it. I was still panicking a bit at that stage. The adrenaline had worn off. I didn't think about the fact it would still be showing in Gavin's sent items until after I'd deleted it. It was stupid. Impulsive. How the hell could a dead man delete his own emails? Then I thought, no, it'll be okay. They won't know when the email was deleted. They might not even discover it ever existed. Either way, there was nothing I could do about it. I had to sit tight.

'And then when you arrested Amie, I wondered what had gone wrong. I wanted to tell you I'd found the emails before that, but I knew that would be a bad idea. I'd be admitting to accessing his emails. It'd look obvious I was trying to prove Amie's innocence and lead you towards Gavin. It was too risky. I knew I'd done the right thing. I knew Amie was innocent and you'd let her go eventually. It was just a case of waiting, waiting until your guys found the emails, looked into Gavin's movements and put two and two together. I knew he couldn't wriggle out of it. Not easily. There was too much. It'd go to court. Easily. Even if a jury cleared him, there'd always be doubt in the back of Amie's mind. And I knew I'd have plenty of time in between to make her mine. But then you started to work it out. And I knew I had to act quickly. I had to do it. For Amie. I always do what's best for her.'

Caroline and Dexter stayed silent for a few moments, taking in and digesting Tom's extraordinary confession. It had been much as Caroline had come to suspect, but hearing it directly from his mouth, laced with his bizarre delusions and reasoning had been quite the ordeal.

'Tom, I'm really sorry,' she said, 'but you can't keep people against their will, no matter how right you believe it to be.'

Tom shrugged. 'What does it matter?' he said. 'I'm done for now. What's the point?' He lifted the camping knife up slightly and looked at it, considering it.

'Tom,' Dexter said, his voice quivering in the cold. 'Tom, look at me, buddy.'

'I'll never have her, will I?' Tom said to Caroline, ignoring him. 'Not after this. Not now. I won't last five minutes in prison. We all know that. This way is easier. Faster.'

'No, Tom,' Caroline said. 'That's not true. Please don't do anything rash.'

'Why not? This is the end. I'll never have her now.'

'That's not true.' Caroline looked at Amie, locking eyes with her, pleading for her to read between the lines.

She'd come to know Amie. She knew she was a stubborn cow who was only out for herself, but Caroline's eyes desperately pleaded for her to see beyond the end of her own nose for once. She needed to at least give Tom the impression that she'd be waiting for him. That he needed to go with the police. That prison time would be worth it. She needed to give him false hope. Caroline didn't know if Amie recognised the message she was trying to send with her eyes, but she knew she had to act quickly. If he took that knife to his neck, he'd stand no chance.

'Tom, please,' she said. 'You haven't lost it all. Not in the slightest. Amie can see how devoted you are to her. How you've dedicated your whole life to protecting her. Can't you, Amie?'

She locked eyes with her again, desperately pleading with her to play along.

Eventually, Amie nodded.

Caroline tried not to make her huge sigh of relief audible. 'Women know when a man will do anything for them, Tom. There's still hope.'

Tears started to glisten in Tom's eyes. 'I need to hear that from her,' he said.

Caroline swallowed. Could Amie be trusted to hold her tongue and play along, just to keep them all safe and ensure justice could be done? If she was honest with herself, she didn't know, but she had no other option. 'Okay,' she said. 'Shall I take the tape off her mouth?'

Tom considered this for a moment, then nodded. 'I'm watching you, though. One wrong move.'

'It's okay, Tom. We're all on the same side here.'

Caroline stepped forward, giving Amie a reassuring

look. As she gently removed the tape, she silently mouthed the word *please*. She stepped back into her previous position, allowing Tom to see Amie's face.

Her phone started to vibrate again. This time, she put her hand in her pocket and pressed the volume-down button, stopping the vibration before Tom noticed it.

'Go on, Amie,' she said. 'Tell him.' Caroline spoke confidently and calmly, but inside she was bricking it. She looked across at Dexter, trying to work out a contingency plan if this all went wrong, but there was none.

'I… Tom,' Amie said, her voice quivering. 'I know you did this for me. I can see that.'

'It was the right thing to do,' Tom replied.

Amie nodded her head desperately. Caroline could see how hard this was for her — how sick she felt at having to go through with the charade — but that she also recognised the importance.

'Tell me,' Tom said, the tears starting to choke him. 'Tell me you'll wait for me.'

'I'll wait for you,' Amie replied, her voice also cracking with emotion, although entirely different ones to his. 'I will. Go with them, Tom. Please.'

'I'll get twenty years. At least.'

Tears were streaming down both their faces.

'I know. I know. You've spent so long waiting for me, Tom. Longer than that. Much longer. It's the least I can do. And you'll be doing it for me.'

'I do everything for you,' he said.

'I know.'

Tom looked at Caroline, then back towards Amie. 'I... I need you to prove it,' he said. 'I need something to take with me.'

'What do you need?' Amie asked, shivering, tearful.

'A kiss. I need a kiss.'

Amie instinctively looked towards Caroline, who'd closed her eyes and clenched her jaw, knowing what Amie's reaction to that request would be.

Caroline looked back at her, hopeful. They were so close. So close to ending this whole ordeal.

Eventually, Amie nodded and Tom stepped forward.

He stooped low, the cold having long seeped into his joints, and planted a long and desperate kiss on her lips.

'You held back,' he said, standing back up and looking at the knife.

'I didn't. I'm cold. I'm frozen solid,' Amie replied desperately, now considering the knife might be intended for her. 'I promise you, Tom. Sweetheart. Kiss me again.'

Tom looked at her for a moment, then kissed her again. He stood back up and walked towards the campfire, each pace slower than the last. Then he looked up at Caroline and Dexter, tossed the knife into the fire and held his arms behind his back.

52

All Caroline wanted was to go home, but the wheels of police procedure meant that wouldn't be possible for a few hours yet. There was the never-ending pile of paperwork that had to be completed first, starting with detailed notes in her policy book on what had happened at Fineshade Wood.

It was always important to get the details down while they were still fresh in the mind, not least because a defence team could quite reasonably try to poke holes in the police's account had it been written down days later, once the details had become fuzzy and the officers' recollections turned hazier.

It was sod's law that these sorts of investigations never came to a head mid-morning or just after lunch. It certainly would've made them easier to write up, without having to work into the early hours just to protect her own backside.

'How's he doing?' she said to Dexter, who'd just come back upstairs from the custody suite.

Dexter shrugged. 'Hard to tell. He's not really saying much. I think he got it all out of his system at the woods.'

'Yeah, tell me about it,' she replied, looking down at the paper in front of her.

'I think he'll be co-operative. Especially if he thinks Amie's going to be waiting for him at the other end.'

'How long before he realises that's not going to happen, though? We'll need to get that confession down in an official statement pretty sharpish.'

'Already on it,' Dexter replied, smiling. 'It's being done as we speak.'

'Brilliant, thanks Dex.'

'You look knackered.'

'Again, thanks Dex. Must be the thought of having to see the Chief Super first thing.'

Dexter smiled. 'Enough to put anyone off their breakfast. Head home and get some kip. Everything looks brighter in the morning. I'll get the paperwork sorted.'

'You sure? You'll be here hours.'

'Nah, won't take that long. Maybe at your age, but I'll fly through it. I'm having tomorrow off, though, yeah?'

'What, despite all your youthful energy and vigour?' Caroline replied, smirking. 'Let's compromise. You can come in at midday.'

Dexter shrugged. 'Suits me. Miss the rush hour at least.'

Caroline stood and stretched, feeling the vertebrae in

her spine clicking. 'Right. Well, in that case I'm off to pop my teeth into a glass of water and make myself a mug of Ovaltine.'

'Mind you don't spill any on your stairlift.'

'Yeah, alright Dex,' Caroline called from the doorway. 'Mind you don't trip down the stairs on your way out.'

53

When Caroline finally arrived home, she was surprised to find the living room light on. Mark was usually in bed long before now, and she hoped this didn't signify another argument was on the cards.

She switched off the engine on her Volvo, opened the door and stepped out onto the driveway. It was a clear night; bitterly cold, but beautiful in its own way, with the stars clearly visible in the night sky. She walked up to the front door and tentatively put her key in the lock, opening the door as quietly as she could. Even though Mark was still up, the boys would be asleep, and her house had a terrible habit of transferring sounds through the walls.

As she stepped into the living room, she saw Mark. He wasn't fully dressed; instead, he was huddled in his dressing gown, his hair askew. It was clear he hadn't waited up, but had been asleep and got up again. There was an old western on TV — a film she didn't recognise, with horses galloping through the dusty desert.

'Mark? Are you okay?'

He turned towards her, and she noticed his eyes were red raw. In the look he gave her, she could see he wasn't upset or angry at her, but at something else entirely. The pleading in his eyes told her he needed her.

'Hey, what's wrong?' she asked, sitting down beside him on the sofa. 'What's happened?'

Mark sniffed, and it was clear to her he'd been crying for some time. 'It's Mum,' he said, his voice cracking. 'She's gone.'

Caroline's heart sank, and in those two words she realised her family had changed forever. Mark had already lost his father and brother to cancer in a short space of time.

'What happened?'

'Joan, her neighbour, called. Apparently Mum was getting into bed tonight and she started to get chest pains. She managed to get to the phone to call the ambulance, but when they got there she'd already gone. They think it was a heart attack.'

Caroline took Mark in her arms. 'Oh no. Sweetheart, I'm so sorry.'

As she held him, she realised just how much she meant those words. She was sorry. She was dreadfully sorry; guilt-ridden at having moved the family from London to Rutland, knowing his mum had only recently lost her husband and a son. Although it had been a joint decision, and one Mark's mum had wholeheartedly endorsed, she felt awful.

'Why didn't she call me, Caz?' he asked, his eyes pleading again. 'I didn't even get to speak to her.'

Caroline put Mark's head on her shoulder and rubbed his back. 'She probably knew. If the ambulance didn't even get there on time with the blues and twos going, there was no way you were going to.'

'But if we were closer.'

'No, you can't think like that,' she replied, for her own benefit as much as his. 'Even in London, it would've taken us far longer to get to hers than an ambulance would.'

'But she might have called me instead.'

'I know. But what good would that have done? You'd have got there later, still found her gone and been left wondering if things might have been different had she only called an ambulance. Or you'd be feeling guilty that you didn't call one for her before leaving. At least this way you know there was nothing anybody could have done. And you get to remember her the way she was her whole life, rather than having that image plaguing you for the rest of yours.'

Mark nodded. She knew he still had the same memories of his dad and brother in their final weeks, their bodies withering away in front of them, as if decomposing before death.

'I need to be there,' he said. 'I… I want to see her, I think. I don't know. Maybe I just need to be in the house. To feel her.'

'I know,' she replied, comforting him. They'd both spent the vast majority of their lives as Londoners, tied to the city. Families, friends, jobs. His mum had been their only major link with London. There was no denying it was the end of an era in so many ways. 'I'm presuming you haven't told the boys?'

Mark shook his head. 'No. I couldn't. I just needed to… I dunno. I needed a bit of time to myself. I needed to process it all first.'

She'd been about to say he should've called her when he found out, when she remembered he'd called her twice while she'd been at Fineshade Wood. She'd silenced the calls, purely because she didn't want to spook Tom, but with the presumption at the back of her mind that Mark was only calling to whinge that she wasn't home and hadn't let him know she'd be late. The guilt set in hard this time, and she began to feel overwhelmed with emotion. She embraced her husband, the two of them crying together, closer than they had been in many months.

54

Sleep had been hard to come by. After having sat up with Mark and getting to bed late, Caroline spent most of the rest of the night worrying about the boys, and how she was going to explain their grandmother's death to them.

When Mark's dad and brother had died, it had been expected. They'd been ill for quite some time, and the family had all had time to prepare — not that it made things any easier. In many ways, it had been harder watching them suffer for so long, going through treatment after treatment, hope after hope, then knowing the end was coming no matter what.

She couldn't imagine what that last stage must feel like. She'd been through the others, of course, but had thankfully never had to come to terms with the knowledge — the absolute certainty — that the end was near. She didn't know how she'd deal with that acceptance, if she could accept it at all. There had been a great many times when it had crossed her mind. More than she cared to remember. But it had always been a worry, a possibility; never the definite outcome.

She felt guilty at equating her illness with what had happened to Mark's dad and brother, but it was unavoidable. If anything, it had helped her to convince herself that the same wouldn't happen to her. Her assumption — her hope — was that lightning couldn't strike thrice.

There was a dull ache at the back of her head — and an increasingly sharp one at the front — as she arrived at work that morning, ready for her meeting with Chief Superintendent Derek Arnold. She'd be pulled up for approaching Tom Mackintosh on her own, without the backup of armed response. There was no doubt about that. But she was comfortable and confident that she could explain her reasoning and certainty that doing things any other way would've resulted in a vastly different outcome. Whether she could put that across succinctly and delicately after so little sleep, though, was another matter.

She knocked on the door of Arnold's office and waited for him to call her in. She stepped inside and sat down.

'Well, good morning,' the Chief Superintendent said, a smile crossing his face. 'Did you get much sleep?'

'Not as much as I would've liked, but then again, when is that not the answer?'

'Indeed. Still, marginally better than a night shift, eh?'

'Marginally,' Caroline replied with a smile. Conversations with Arnold always seemed to feel slightly stilted. She could never quite work him out, and there was often an air of something approaching awkwardness.

'So, how's everything going otherwise? You seem to be recovering well.'

'I am, I think. Still not fully there yet, but I don't think I'm far off.'

'Good, good. Have you had the... you know... the all clear?'

'Not quite. In remission, hopefully. I should find out any day now if the operation got everything or if it's grown back since. Then they're talking about scans and checkups every few months before they're happy to sign me off completely.'

Arnold raised his eyebrows and murmured to himself. 'Blimey. Quite the journey, eh? Still, fingers crossed we're on the home straight now.'

'Fingers crossed, sir.'

'And a good result on Operation Cruickshank. In the end.'

Caroline forced a smile. She understood the not-so-hidden meaning of those last three words. 'Yes, in the end,' she said, feeling an immediate need to justify herself but trying to find the words to do so diplomatically. 'It wasn't a conventional case, by any means. Far from straightforward and with a number of complicating factors, so I think the whole team can be very proud of what we've managed to achieve in a relatively short space of time.'

Arnold nodded as he looked at her. 'Indeed. Indeed.

And while we're on the subject of unconventionality... I think you know what I'm going to say.'

'Fineshade Wood?'

'Fineshade Wood.'

'I know,' Caroline replied. 'To be honest, it was one of those situations where a judgment call had to be made. Knowing what we knew of Mackintosh and the circumstances as a whole, we judged it would be far less risky to go in and talk to him rather than having an armed mob turn up.'

'Or a selection of highly-trained officers, as most people would call them.'

'I appreciate that, sir. And I agree. But I'm looking at this through the eyes of the man with the kidnap victim and the weapon. From what we knew of him, and of Amie Tanner, we came to the conclusion that it was the best way of resolving things without further injury or loss of life.'

'We?' Arnold asked.

'Sorry. Me. The decision was entirely mine.'

'Okay. We've got trained negotiators for that, you know. It's no good risking your own safety.'

'I know. But we had an existing relationship with him. I judged that would be a big advantage, considering the circumstances. And I think that judgement has been borne out to be the right one, all things considered.'

Arnold looked at her for a moment, then gave a single, solitary nod of acceptance. 'Okay,' he said. 'You do realise I'm saying all this because these are the questions that'll be asked of me. I've got to answer to my superiors, too.'

'Of course.'

'For what it's worth, I think you made the right call. And I'll be passing that up the food chain.'

'Thank you, sir. That means a lot.'

Arnold smiled. 'In fact, there's something else I want to speak to them about. I may as well tell you now. I'm planning on nominating you for a special commendation.'

Caroline was stunned into silence. She felt sure Arnold would at least question her methods, if not rip her a new one, but she certainly hadn't expected this. 'Oh. Wow. Thank you, sir. It's an honour.'

'No guarantees, of course. It's not technically up to me; I can only nominate you. But in my experience these things tend to go through without a hitch. Provided you haven't slept with the Assistant Chief Constable's wife or anything.'

'Not that I can recall, sir. What's her name?'

'Susan. I wouldn't recommend it. She strikes me as a biter.'

'I'll bear it in mind, sir. I wouldn't want to spoil my chances.'

Arnold smiled again. 'And proper closure on the Russell Speakman case, too. That's not to be sniffed at.'

'Yeah, that was a handy little bonus. I'm afraid I can't really take any credit for that one, though.'

'Oh, I don't know. From what I understand, it was your tenacity and probing that flushed Ruby whatsherface out into the open.'

'Ruby Clifford. And I'm not sure about that. She was

racked with guilt, the poor thing, even though she hadn't really done anything. At least now her conscience is clear. And, as you say, it gives the case proper closure.'

'Good. Good. Now, on to more important matters. I hear on the grapevine that a few of you are planning on having some celebratory drinks later. Is that correct?'

Caroline winced inwardly. Arnold's tone told her he wasn't exactly best pleased with what he'd heard. 'Well, it was mentioned briefly that one or two might stop off for a quick half on the way home. But nothing heavy, especially not for those working tomorrow.'

'Ah, I think you misunderstand me, DI Hills,' Arnold said. 'You've got every right to celebrate and enjoy yourselves. That wasn't really my question.'

'Sorry, sir,' Caroline said, feeling surer than ever that she'd never truly understand the man. 'What is the question then?'

Arnold's smile returned, and this time it was beaming. 'Have you got room for one more?'

55

Although Caroline had never been a big pub-goer, she found the low rumble of conversation and the occasional chinking of glasses to be strangely comforting and relaxing. On the whole, she couldn't stand background noise, but there was something about pubs that was different.

Pubs in London had an altogether different vibe. She'd rarely visited any of the pubs in and around Cricklewood. From what she could make out, they'd been either dive bars, extortionately priced gastropubs or even more extortionately priced craft beer houses made to cater for the growing hipster community. One of the many things she'd been glad to discover in Rutland was that the traditional British pub was alive and well — and few did it in greater style than the Wheatsheaf, just a stone's throw from work and a short meander home should it be necessary to leave her car, which more often than not tended to be the case.

It would be fair to say the dynamic had shifted slightly

with the addition of Derek Arnold to the celebratory drinks but, to give him his due, he seemed to be trying his best to fit in and not wear his superior-officer hat too obviously. On the contrary, Caroline found herself more concerned with her own team.

Almost as if he could read her mind, Aidan looked up from his phone and forced a smile. He'd seemed distracted the whole evening, constantly checking his phone and responding to text messages.

She'd noticed Sara had been quieter than usual over the past few days too, and through everything else that'd been going on she hadn't pieced it all together. When she thought back, it was obvious. She'd taken the revelation about Aidan being gay far harder than she'd initially let on. Sara had more or less worked it out for herself, and had told Caroline she'd had an inkling, but it was now clear that she'd been clinging onto the hope she'd been wrong for far too long.

Sara had always been one of the quieter officers she'd met. She was calm, collected, dedicated and studious. But Caroline felt shamed that she didn't know much more about her. The chat they'd had over coffee in The Daily Grind had been a revelation in many ways, but it still hadn't escaped her notice that she knew precious little about such an important member of her team. If she was honest with herself, she didn't know all that much about any of them, with perhaps the partial exception of Dexter, who she'd spent much more time with, and who seemed only too happy to share details about his life.

'So. Anyone got any holidays planned this year?' she asked, before realising how cringeworthy the question sounded.

'Nothing planned,' Dexter replied. 'Might sort out something last minute.'

A rumble of laughter ran through the group at the inside joke. As wonderful as last-minute holidays sounded, the succession of ever-changing shift patterns meant planning ahead was key.

'How about you, Aidan?' Caroline asked.

Aidan looked up from his phone, for what must have been only the second time that evening. 'Huh? Sorry.'

'Holidays. Got any planned?'

'Oh. No, not really. We might try and get a few days in Devon or Cornwall in the summer. See how it goes.'

The wording hadn't been lost on Caroline. 'We? Have you kissed and made up, then?'

'Hmmm? Oh. No. No, we haven't. This is somebody new.'

Caroline nodded. 'Ah. Is that who you've been typing out *War and Peace* to for the last hour and a half?'

'Sorry.'

'Honestly, it's fine,' she said, laughing. 'I remember when I used to like Mark. Someone local, is it?'

'Yeah. Very local, actually. As in about-ten-houses-further-down-Northgate local.'

Caroline glanced across at Sara. She was a difficult person to read, but she'd been subdued for days anyway, and Aidan was clearly distracted and mentally elsewhere.

Besides which, the couple of pints of Tiger Caroline'd sunk had loosened her up a little.

'Well why not join us?' she said, the issue of getting to know her team personally being very much on her mind. It'd be good to meet Aidan's new man from the off.

'Are you sure?' Aidan asked, as if trying to work out if the offer was genuine.

'Of course,' Caroline replied. 'The more the merrier.'

'Are you going away anywhere this year, sir?' Sara asked Derek Arnold, in a clear attempt to change the conversation.

'Well, my wife and I tend to go to St Lucia for a couple of weeks. There's a nice little spot we've been to a few times.'

'Christ, I bet you wish you were joining Aidan in Cornwall, don't you?' Caroline said, chuckling.

Arnold smiled. 'Not much, no.'

'Colour me jealous,' Dexter said. 'I was hoping to do a pilgrimage to Antigua this year, but I can't see that happening.'

'You still got family there?' Arnold asked.

'Some. Fairly distant ones I've either never met or only met once as a child. We went back once in the holidays when I was at school. I was probably only about six, so I barely remember it, but I remember thinking it was my idea of paradise. It's definitely made holidays since feel much more mundane.'

All the talk of holidays made Caroline yearn to get away. Mark and the boys needed it just as much as she did, especially after the last year or two. She told herself she'd pop into Savvi Travel on the high street over the weekend and pick up some details. She could never get on with booking holidays over the internet. She was sure it was great if you knew exactly where and when you wanted to go, but travel websites didn't seem to cope well with searches like 'somewhere hot, with a swimming pool, in the next twelve months'.

Twenty minutes later, and with the glasses almost empty, Caroline had completely forgotten that Aidan's new boyfriend was due to join them. So she was more than a little surprised when the door opened and a stunning young woman came in, looked around, spotted Aidan and walked straight over.

Aidan stood and kissed her on the cheek, putting his arm around her. 'Guys, this is Keira. Caroline, my DI. Dex and Sara. And I'm not quite sure whether I'm meant to call you sir, or...'

'Derek's more than fine in the pub,' Arnold said, smiling, oblivious to everything that had been said between Aidan, Sara and Caroline. 'Pleasure to meet you, Keira.'

Caroline looked over at Sara, whose demeanour had dropped several octaves, despite trying to put a brave face on it.

'Do you want a drink?' Aidan asked Keira, gesturing towards the bar.

'It's alright. It's my round,' Caroline said. 'Actually, Aidan, you can give me a hand.'

They went over to the bar and placed their order.

'She seems nice,' Caroline said.

'She is, yeah.'

'And female.'

Aidan looked at her for a moment. 'Uh, yes. Well spotted.'

'So, you're...'

'Bisexual. Yes. Is that an issue?'

'No. No, of course not. Obviously not. I mean, I thought you were gay, so, you know.'

'Sorry to disappoint,' Aidan quipped, smiling.

Caroline turned her head towards their table. Keira was proving to be as bright and bubbly as she'd first seemed and was already holding court, engaging the others as she told a witty anecdote. Caroline could see Sara was trying to be polite and friendly, but there was something else underneath. Disappointment. Confusion. Regret.

'Is something up?' Aidan asked.

'No. No, nothing at all,' Caroline replied, taking her card from her purse. 'All good.'

'With Sara, I mean. She's been a bit funny recently.'

Caroline tried to think of the best way to answer. 'I think she's alright. I've not asked.'

'I have,' Aidan replied. 'She said she was fine, but I don't believe her. Might be worth keeping an eye on her.'

'Yeah,' Caroline said, looking back over at Sara. 'Yeah, I will.'

'I've got a lot of time for her. She's a nice girl.'

'Sara?'

'Yeah. Why, do you not think so?'

'Of course. Yes, sorry, no, that's not what I meant. Sorry.'

Aidan gave her an odd look. 'I don't know how confused I'm meant to be right now, but I think I'd score pretty highly.'

Me too, Caroline thought.

They carried the drinks back and set them down on the table. As Aidan sat next to Keira and put his arm round her, Sara shuffled uncomfortably.

'Back in a sec,' she said. 'Just got to nip to the loo.'

Caroline watched her leave, gave it a moment or two, then stood up too. 'Actually, I should probably go as well, before I get too comfy.'

With the others seemingly oblivious, she followed Sara to the ladies', where she found her leaning on a sink, looking in the mirror.

'I know this probably doesn't help,' Caroline said, 'but I didn't know either. I just assumed... Well, you know.'

'I knew I should've just come out and asked him.'

'I dunno, Sara. They could've known each other a while for all we know. It might not've made a difference.'

Sara shook her head. 'Less than a week. While you were at the bar she made a point of telling us what a "whirlwind romance" it'd been.'

Caroline looked at her, wishing she could do something to make her feel better. She'd never seen Sara quite so upset or annoyed. 'If it means anything, these sorts of things tend to fizzle out just as quickly as they started. The slow burners are the long lasters, as they say.'

'I doubt that. I mean, look at her. She's perfect for him. She's bright, she's bubbly, she's bloody stunning. It's probably a good job I didn't say anything to him. Would've been even more embarrassing if I had.'

'Don't think like that,' Caroline replied, far from sure as to how she should be thinking.

Sara looked at herself in the mirror, and Caroline watched as she snapped herself out of her mind, as if switching on the Sara Henshaw she knew everyone else wanted to see. In that moment, Caroline realised this was a woman who had her internal struggles and battles, but who kept them all well hidden from everyone else. In that respect, she saw much of herself in Sara.

'Come on,' she said, putting a hand on Sara's shoulder. 'Let's go back and have a drink. If we get a few down Kiera she might out herself as a closet arsehole and force Aidan to ditch her.'

Sara lifted one corner of her mouth into a half-smile. 'Maybe we can get her to admit she's a Nottingham Forest fan. That should do it.'

'You mind your language, DC Henshaw. Come on.'

As they made their way back to the table and sat down, Caroline began to tune out the conversation. It joined the background hum of the pub, the atmosphere of life and community she was coming to enjoy so much. And as she watched her small but loyal team toasting another job well done, she realised her own role was evolving.

EPILOGUE

Caroline sat down in the consultant's room and tried to gauge what he was about to say from the look on his face. He was a difficult man to read — deliberately, she imagined. She knew from her own job that it was often a good idea to keep one's cards close to one's chest, and to get the opportunity to present the information properly and professionally, without undue emotion.

Mark held her hand, squeezing it tight, her constant source of strength and support.

'Okay, so we're here for your scan results,' the consultant said, as if he'd expected Caroline to bring them with her.

'Yes. The MRI,' she replied.

'Indeed. I won't keep you hanging on — it looks like good news. The surgery appears to have removed all the cancerous tissue, and there are no signs of any regrowth showing on the scan.'

Although the consultant continued talking, Caroline didn't hear a word. Her head filled with so many emotions, she could barely identify them, never mind process them. Sheer joy took the lead, along with an enormous sense of relief. There was regret at everything she'd had to go through, anger that it had shaped her life so much and an unfortunate sense of guilt for those who hadn't been so fortunate as to hear the words she'd just heard. And then there was Mark, and everything it had put him through.

'Now, I understand it's probably quite an emotional thing to hear,' the consultant said, Caroline desperately trying to focus on his words. 'Do you need a minute?'

'No. No, I'm fine. Just a huge relief,' she replied, Mark kissing her on the head.

'From a medical point of view, I'm delighted to be able to say you're now officially in remission. But there's still quite a bit of aftercare to happen. We're going to continue to monitor you, just to make sure there's no regrowth or any symptoms cropping up elsewhere. That'll involve regular checkups, scans and monitoring. It also means that on the unlikely off-chance something does crop up, we're able to deal with it much more quickly, before it gets out of hand.'

As the consultant spoke, Caroline felt her thoughts drifting again, and was thankful for Mark being here with her. Her head was all over the place, but she knew he'd pick up the details. He always had. Always would.

A short while later, Caroline and Mark stepped outside

and into the fresh air. Caroline breathed in deeply, savouring the sensation. There would be many more breaths to come, and she was going to make sure she enjoyed every single one of them.

She took off her scarf and unzipped her coat. It had been a bitterly cold morning when they'd arrived at the hospital, but the sun was now out, bathing everything in an energising yellow light.

She watched as the last remnants of frost and ice dripped from the railings, forming glistening puddles on the floor. After a long, hard winter, it seemed as though spring had finally sprung. It was shaping up to be a beautiful day.

WANT MORE?

I hope you enjoyed *In Cold Blood*.

If you did, you'll be pleased to hear the Rutland crime series continues with *Kiss of Death*.

If you want to be the first to hear about new books — and get a couple of free short stories in the meantime — head to:

adamcroft.net/vip-club

Two free short stories will be sent to you straight away, and you'll be the first to hear about new releases.

For more information, visit my website: **adamcroft.net**

ACKNOWLEDGMENTS

As I write these opening words of the acknowledgements, I'm watching the snow fall outside my office window. When I started writing the book, I had no idea if we were going to have a cold winter or a mild one. Not that it mattered: it's a fictional book with fictional characters working for a fictional police force. But even though the world of my books is largely made-up, it carries on in a roughly parallel timeline with the real world — albeit one where things like global pandemics can be safely ignored and forgotten about.

In any case, the theme of cold was one that stuck with me throughout the writing of this book. Perhaps it's a natural result of everyone having spent a year isolated from their family and friends. Maybe it was my own prescient foreknowledge about the cold weather we were going to have (and I'm totally claiming god-like wisdom here). More likely, it was my own fatalistic outlook on the world. Either way, a lot of things in this book were bloody cold, and I'm not just talking about the weather.

When I started writing this book, it was a mild autumn. We hadn't even had a frost. I genuinely worried that in writing about a cold winter, I was virtually guaranteeing we'd all be walking around in shorts in February and that I'd look quite the tit — and I'm not just referring to the shorts. Thankfully, Old Mother Nature vindicated me.

But, even though I'm most thankful to Zeus and Michael Fish (is he still going? I know Zeus is getting on a bit), there are a number of other, less weather-controlling people I must thank.

As always, Graham Bartlett has been an invaluable resource in helping me make the policing aspect of my books as accurate as possible. The rather dull nature of real-life policing does mean procedural accuracy must often fall in line behind story. After all, the Rutland crime series being mostly set in plush police offices in Nottingham or Derby with a cast of hundreds wouldn't have quite the same appeal.

Simon Cole, Chief Constable of Leicestershire Police, was incredibly helpful with information on mobile ANPR and helping me out of yet another sticky plot point. Thank you, Simon.

Huge thanks go to Jon Brocklebank, Head Gardener at Barnsdale Gardens for all his help and assistance for the information on forcing roses into out-of-season growth. If anyone is reading this (why would you?) and you've never visited Barnsdale Gardens, you absolutely must. It's much cheaper than a spa, a whole lot more therapeutic, and you don't need to strip down to your pants if you really don't want to.

Horticultural thanks also go to Adam Frost for information on the Black Baccara rose. Frosty, I apologise for Caroline's comments — I couldn't resist it. Those beers are definitely on me now.

One of the things I've been keen to portray most accurately in this series is Caroline's struggle with cancer. For this, my thanks go once again to my friend and nurse (in the general sense — she's not *my* nurse) Jo Clarke, who is rather too enthusiastically interested in cancer for me to feel comfortable speaking to her any more than once every couple of months.

One or two readers quite fairly pointed out that the police wouldn't risk having a seriously ill officer on duty, and that there's a huge duty of care from the police service. I hope no-one thought I was implying otherwise. Again, this is a situation where sometimes story leads and everything else follows. Caroline's someone who tends to keep the severity of her own issues very much to herself. In any case, the books would be really rather dull if they consisted of a few hundred pages of Caroline sitting at home with a hot water bottle, watching *Homes Under the Hammer*.

On feedback, one resident did contact me to inform me that the viaduct is — *actually, I think you'll find, Mr Croft* — in Northamptonshire. Although most of it is indeed in the fair county of Northants, the northern stretch of the viaduct that divides Seaton Meadows is very much in Rutland. Honestly. Look on a map.

You might have spotted in the blurb on the back of the book that I refer to the viaduct here as Welland Viaduct.

Prior to the book's launch, a couple of people contacted me to tell me the viaduct is *actually* called Harringworth Viaduct, and it was clear I knew nothing of the local area, having given myself away with such a death-penalty-inducing error. As you'll have just read (unless you've skipped to this bit), locals in the book — as in real life — refer to it as Harringworth Viaduct. I'll let you in on a little secret: so do I. Most people do. Unfortunately, the majority of official sources seem to agree its 'proper' name is Welland Viaduct. I know. I know. I don't like it either. But with the books being sold in numerous countries around the world, it felt right that the blurb should use the viaduct's more official name, and for the characters in the book to use the local sobriquet.

On the subject of dead bodies and viaducts, I need to thank Dr Samantha Pickles, Senior Lecturer in Forensic Science at the University of Bedfordshire, for all the help and information she provided. If you ever need to know what state a dead body would be in after spending a few hours under a freezing cold viaduct, Sam's your girl.

To Lucy, Beverley, Jacob, Joanne, Helen and my mum for reading early copies of the book and not laughing too much while they offered their feedback — thank you.

To Nick Castle for a fantastic cover — thank you.

Thanks also to Jim and Xander for being top-drawer assistants and general dogsbodies. I couldn't do half the things I do without those chaps keeping me on the straight and narrow.

If you've not yet listened to the audiobooks of the

Rutland series, you really must. They're absolutely fantastic. Enormous thanks go to Andy Nyman for bringing the books to life with his narration, and to Craig and the whole team at WF Howes for making it possible and being kind enough to publish the series in audiobook.

Thanks also to Rosie, Jonathan and everyone else in the film & TV department at PFD for all the work you're doing on trying to get the series on TV. It's been such a challenging year for that industry, and I appreciate everything you're doing.

Huge thanks must go to all of the local, independent retailers in the East Midlands who've been supporting the series by stocking signed paperbacks. After the tough year they've had, nothing gives me more pleasure than seeing them do a roaring trade.

I'm absolutely certain there are people I've missed. Quite a lot of them, I imagine. It would be really handy if I kept a list of people I needed to thank while writing each book, so I could make sure I remember them all when it comes to writing the acknowledgements. To be fair, this time I did at least start a list, but then I forgot about the list itself, which made the whole plan rather redundant. If your name is missing from this rambling list of acknowledgements and you're absolutely *certain* I don't think you're a pillock, this one's for you: THANK YOU.

A SPECIAL THANK YOU TO MY PATRONS

Thank you to everyone who's a member of my Patreon program. Active supporters get a number of benefits, including the chance of having a character named after them in my books. In this book, PC Vickie Hughes was named after a Patreon supporter.

With that, I'd like to give my biggest thanks to my small but growing group of readers who are currently signed up as Patreon supporters at the time of writing: Alexier Mayes, Andy Jeens, Angela Pepper, Ann Sidey, Anne Davies, Barbara Tallis, Carla Powell, Cheryl Hill, Claire Blincoe, Claire Evans, Daniel MacLagan, Dawn Godsall, Dawn Philip, Emiliana Anna Perrone, Estelle Golding, Francis W Markus, Gordon Aldred, Gordon Bonser, Helen Brown, Helen Weir, Jay Vernalls, Jean Wright, Jeanette Moss, Jenny Must, Josephine Graham, Julie Devonald Cornelius, Karina Gallagher, Kerry Hammond, Kerry Robb, Kirstin Anya Wallace, Leigh Hansen, Linda Anderson, Lisa Bayliss, Lisa Lewkowicz, Lisa-marie Thompson, Lynne Davis, Lynne Lester-George, Mandy Davies, Mary Fortey, Maureen Hutchings, Mrs J Budnik-Hillier, Nigel M Gibbs, Paul Wardle, Paula Holland, Peter Tottman, Rachel, Ruralbob, Sally Catling,

Sally-Anne Coton, Sam, Samantha Harris, Sarah Hughes, Sharon Oakes, Sheanne Lovatt, Sim Croft, Sue, Susan Bingham, Susan Cox, Susan Fiddes, Sylvia Crampin, Tracey Clark, Tremayne Alflatt and Vickie Hughes. You're all absolute superstars.

If you're interested in becoming a patron, please head over to patreon.com/adamcroft. Your support is hugely appreciated.

HAVE YOU LISTENED TO THE RUTLAND AUDIOBOOKS?

The Rutland crime series is now available in audiobook format, narrated by Leicester-born **Andy Nyman** (Peaky Blinders, Unforgotten, Star Wars).

The series is available from all good audiobook retailers and libraries now, published by W.F. Howes on their QUEST and Clipper imprints.

W.F. Howes are one of the world's largest audiobook publishers and have been based in Leicestershire since their inception.

W.F. HOWES LTD
QUEST

ADAM CROFT

With over two million books sold to date, Adam Croft is one of the most successful independently published authors in the world, having sold books in over 120 different countries.

In February 2017, Amazon's overall Author Rankings briefly placed Adam as the most widely read author in the world at that moment in time, with J.K. Rowling in second place.

Adam is considered to be one of the world's leading experts on independent publishing and has been featured on BBC television, *BBC Radio 4*, *BBC Radio 5 Live*, the *BBC World Service*, *The Guardian*, *The Huffington Post*, *The Bookseller* and a number of other news and media outlets.

In March 2018, Adam was conferred as an Honorary Doctor of Arts, the highest academic qualification in the UK, by the University of Bedfordshire in recognition of his services to literature.

Adam presents the regular crime fiction podcast *Partners in Crime* with fellow bestselling author and television actor Robert Daws.